TENDER PURDY

MYSTERIES

Tender's Top Secret Case

RICHARD P. HARRINGTON

To my Lord and Savior, Jesus Christ.

Books are Keys

Table of Contents

Prologue

David and I had just put Tender to bed, as we did every night, then we headed down the hall, sat on the couch and cuddled. As usual I did most of the talking. I sometimes wondered if we had driven across the country, and I never said a word if David would be happy. "David, can you believe it has been over a year and a half since Tender tricked us into adopting her?" I looked at David and smiled. "I remember the day like it was yesterday. I pulled up close to Alex and Loriann's house and grabbed Anne's gift out of my car. Just then a cab pulled up and the driver got out and handed me a small box and said, 'for you ma'am.' A little girl hopped out of the backseat and grabbed my hand. If she had not been holding my hand, then I would have stopped the driver and talked to him. Also, I recently recalled that the cab had no license plate. That is so suspicious. I tried talking to the little girl as she pulled me into the house, but she was chattering the whole time. 'I love parties, don't you? I can't wait to have cake. What gift did you get for the birthday girl?"

"I thought she was a friend of Anne's and that her mom would just pick her up later. I didn't realize that Loriann did not recognize her when she asked me who I had brought with me. I never got to answer her as she rushed off to welcome another guest. If I had been a better detective back then I would have investigated more about the whole event, but I didn't think to do that."

"Now I realize that our little genius knew to distract me as she ran off to play with Anne so I would think she was a friend of hers. She tricked me that day." I looked over to David again to see what he was thinking.

"I can believe she tricked you that day. And I know it was all part of her plan to have us adopt her," David said. He was staring out into space and then added, "I know her biological mother wanted us to adopt Tender, so I think they planned the whole thing out. I cannot imagine not growing up with a loving family, so I understand her mom wanting her to have parents and not end up in an orphanage like you and her biological mother did. I believe we are truly blessed to have her choose us to be her parents." David reached over and hugged me as tears trickled down my cheeks. "Just look at the amazing life she has lived already, she solves so many cases, but none more than helping the FBI find 59 missing girls." David said.

"I was amazed at how she solved the case of the "Real Estate Killer." I chimed in. "Let's face it David, she has fulfilled her birth mother's wishes that she helps at least one person in trouble every year. I believe Tender would say her favorite case was finding Anthony Ricci. So, what is our goal as parents this year for our little girl?" I smiled at David.

"One think bothers me. Why is Tender so obsessed with Vicky Smith? Ever since we discovered sixty girls went missing, she only focused on her?" David noted.

"I believe it is because she is deaf, and that she went to school at the same time as I did." I said.

"Yes, that makes sense." David responded. "As her dad I would love to see the three of us take a vacation. We have spent so much time asking Tender to help us, except for a few days camping, she only knows school and solving mysteries." David said.

"Ok I would love it if we could get away for a

week with no case to solve, now let's get to bed it's late." As we headed down the hall holding hands, I put my head on David's shoulder, and thought about our amazing daughter.

ONE

Flight of the Hornets

It was Saturday night, David, Tender, and I were enjoying our weekly movie and popcorn night with Mary, David's sister, and Mary's boyfriend, Richard. After the movie, Tender looked at Mary and Richard, "I have a job I need you both to do, and it is going to be difficult. It's about the case with the missing girls and Vicky Smith" said Tender.

"Yes, she is the deaf girl, right?" answered Mary. "The FBI found the other missing girls, but they couldn't find her. We were working on that case before the town hall meeting last week."

"She was the young girl that your mom helped with her homework when they were both at St. Paul's," Richard answered proudly. As always, he was pleased to be contributing to the case. "Doesn't she have a photographic memory like you?"

"Yes. I need to find her, first because she is deaf, and second because I have a bad feeling about her. I believe she is in trouble and is crying out," said Tender. Her eyes were tearing up, and she wiped her eyes with her sleeve.

"Where do we start?" asked Richard, putting his arm around Tender.

"Go to the library and find every school for deaf children in the United States. Then contact them and ask if they have enrolled any new students in the last few months," Tender instructed them.

"Tender, if they are a school for the deaf, how will they answer the phone?" asked Mary, concerned.

"Most schools for the deaf have an office administrator who can hear as well as use sign language," Tender explained.

"Okay, but what if they don't employ such a person?" Richard asked. He nervously ran his fingers through his hair.

"We can contact the local FBI office and see if they are willing to send an agent who speaks and signs," Tender said confidently.

It was getting late, so David took Mary and Richard home. On Sunday morning, David and I were feeling under the weather, so we all stayed home and rested.

By Monday morning, everyone was feeling a lot

better except Tender. She now had a slight fever, so she was going to stay with me at work instead of going to school for the day. Once we arrived at Bismarck police headquarters, Chief Purdy (who was also David's uncle) informed David and me that we were to report to FBI headquarters for a new case.

We decided to have our breakfast in the FBI cafeteria, as no one was hungry when we first woke up. As soon as we entered the building, Tender ran over to the front desk, where Big John, a large black man, was sitting. As he bent down to receive her hug, he frowned and put his hand on her forehead. "Tender, you are hot. Are you sick?" he asked anxiously.

"I have a slight fever, but I feel fine," she smiled up at him.

"Well, I hope so, but don't overdo it today. So, Special Agent Tender Purdy, what brings you to us early this morning?" Big John asked, using Tender's full title.

Tender enjoyed entering FBI headquarters and being addressed as Special Agent Tender Purdy. "Chief Purdy informed us to report to Director Lance Steward's office. Big John, we are heading to the cafeteria for breakfast. Do you want to join us?" Tender asked.

"I had breakfast already, and I am on duty, but make sure you see me on your way out for one of my famous rainbow pops," Big John replied with a wink. Then he shot a warning look at David, who was always trying to find a way to get his hands on one of those pops.

"I will!" Tender replied with a thumbs-up as we headed for breakfast.

"Mom, I think Dad, might die if we take any longer to get food," Tender laughed. David had been tugging on my blouse for us to hurry up while Tender talked with Big John. I playfully slapped his hand.

"David, calm down." I said. We hurried to the cafeteria and got ourselves breakfast. As usual, David ate the most.

Once breakfast was finished, we headed to Director Lance's office.

"Good morning, Purdys," Director Lance said with a smile, as we entered his office.

"Good morning, Director Lance," David said. "I understand you have a case for us?"

"Yes, I do. I have a very strange case, which has us all baffled. Let's head over to Agent Dwayne Sisson's investigation room."

As we entered the room, over twenty agents were already there, sitting around and waiting for our arrival .

"Good morning, Agent Sisson," we all greeted him.

"Good morning, Purdys; it sure is good to see you here. Well, let's get started. In the last month, we have had six people die from hornet stings."

Agent Sisson started pulling up pictures of the hornet stings. Tender immediately started looking at them with great interest.

Agent Sisson looked at her quizzically. "Tender, can you explain how six people—four men and two women—could die from hornet stings?" Agent Sisson asked after a while.

Tender kept looking at the pictures of the hornet stings. It was so quiet in the room that you could hear a pin drop. Finally, she said, "First, these pictures are of killer hornets, called *Vespa Mandarina*. They are the world's largest hornets, and they can grow up to two inches long. They only come from Asia. They entered the U.S. in wooden crates."

Director Lance wanted to know how the hornet venom affected humans.

Tender replied, "The venom attacks the nervous system. Once you are stung, you will die within twenty-four hours, as the venom is ten times more deadly than any other venom." Tender looked at the map showing where all the victims died. "However, these six people were murdered, not stung."

There were gasps around the room. "Tender, how do you know that?" asked Agent Sisson in amazement.

"*Vespa Mandarina* stings like a machine gun; the victims would have gotten hundreds of stings in just seconds. However, each of these victims has only one puncture wound. My guess is that these murders were done by a venom ring used by killers to poison their victims. What's more, there has never been a sighting of a *Vespa Mandarina* in any of the states on this map."

Tender paused for a moment, then she added, "We are looking for a woman assassin."

"Why a woman?" asked Director Lance, looking at Tender quizzically.

"A male assassin would never use such a complicated murder device," chuckled Tender. "I would guess she is petite and married with children, and she would prefer not to witness the death of her victims. Now I need to see what you have discovered about the victims," Tender went on, with a glance at Agent Sisson.

Agent Sisson exhaled and ran his hands through his hair. Then he said, "Unfortunately, we don't have much to go on. All the victims had different occupations. Two of them had criminal records, but the other four had nothing outstanding to report."

Tender looked at the map and asked, "Is this where they all lived?"

"No, none of them lived where they died," Agent Sisson responded. He leaned back in his chair.

"We need to find out how or why they ended up where they died," said Tender, her brows furrowed. "We need to split into groups to solve this. Director Lance, it's time to give out assignments."

One agent was assigned to each victim, with instructions to investigate why they were traveling out of state. Then Tender, David, and I headed to the FBI cafeteria for a break. Director Lance came along.

"Tender, what do you think about this case?" he asked with a smile.

"I do think everybody makes at least one mistake, and she already made one," Tender said thoughtfully, sipping some orange juice.

"Do you mean in the way she administered the venom?" Director Lance pressed.

"Yes. And the fact that she murdered too many victims in a short amount of time."

"Why would that matter?" Director Lance looked puzzled.

"Most assassins are careful not to repeat the same crime too many times in a row. It means she needed money quickly," Tender said, finishing her juice. She looked at me hopefully. "Mom, can I have some more juice?" she asked.

"Not right now, darling," I responded with a smile. "One glass is enough, plus it's time for us to be getting back to the investigation room."

After our break, we went back to the investigation room to see if the agents had discovered anything. No one had found any reason for each victim's trip. It was surprising, however, that all six were married, but none of their spouses knew why they had gone away.

Tender gave each of the agents a task. "I think I know what happened, but I need more information," she said. "I believe each of these victims travels to these locations quite often. We also need to find out if any of them applied for a divorce recently. We'll come back tomorrow to see what you all have uncovered. But for now, I need to go home. I don't feel so well," Tender said with a tired sigh.

I looked at Tender and saw she had gone pale. We quickly got our things and left to go home. On the way out she didn't even want her rainbow pop. David put his hand out, "Big John, you can trust me. I will give it to Tender later." He smiled.

"David Purdy, do you take me for a fool? As soon as you get in the car you will ask Tender if she wants her rainbow pop. When she says no, you

12

will eat it." Then he repeated, "Agents only or find girl number sixty."

Tender poked her dad and said, "Yes let's find Vicky Smith."

Once we were in the car, I asked Tender, "Darling, are you okay? Let me feel your forehead. We shouldn't have stayed so long." I put my hand on Tender's forehead anxiously. It still felt hot.

"I feel okay, Mom, but to tell the truth, this case bothers me. It's awful to know a mother could do such a thing," Tender said quietly. She had her eyes closed and was resting her head on the back seat. "Are you sure we shouldn't pass on this case?" I suggested. "You say you're fine, but you don't look fine to me." "No! We must stop this evil woman. I hope the children who are left without a parent have someone close to care for them," Tender opened her eyes and looked pleadingly at me.

The next day, the weather was awful, with heavy rain and high winds. I was so glad I had negotiated an indoor parking space at FBI headquarters for Tender. We also decided to get breakfast in the cafeteria two days in a row.

Once we were there, around mouthfuls of bacon and eggs, David said. "Tender, your mom and I are both concerned that this case is getting to be too much since you are not feeling well." He put his fork down on the table and looked over at Tender. She was pushing some fruit around her plate. I noticed she hadn't eaten very much. She looked up quickly at David.

"Please, Dad and Mom. I love helping people, and I understand there are bad moms and dads in the world. I know God is using me to help stop these bad people from hurting anyone else. Even in the Bible, God punished the wicked women and men, and even children for doing wrong."

David and I looked at each other in resignation. David sighed and said, "Okay, we will keep working on this case. It's just that we love you so much, and we don't want you to be upset."

We went back upstairs to hear all the agents give their reports on the case. At the end, Agent Sisson summarized, "To track down the 'hornet killer,' we have followed up with the next of kin of the victims. We discovered that they all traveled to locations where they had family. However, they did not stay with their relatives."

Tender nodded. "Yes, I guessed they would not stay with relatives for this kind of trip. We also need to know if they flew in coach or first class."

David, Tender, and I began to review the files on the victims. David noticed they were all very wealthy. "Well, now we know the killer's motive." I exclaimed.

"Yes, we do," replied Tender. She slumped down in her chair. I thought she looked sad again, but when she saw I was looking at her carefully, she quickly straightened up and smiled at me.

After studying the files for almost four hours, we headed to the cafeteria for lunch. David was enjoying the all-you-can-eat buffet. I am always amazed at how he never gains weight; I contribute this to the amount of time he spends in the police gym.

After lunch, the agents were back to give us further reports. All the agents reported the same results. Every time a victim flew to the location, they flew in coach, but on this particular flight, they flew first class. The agents also reported, as Tender had surmised, that none of their family members knew they had been in town.

Tender then said, "I think I know who the 'hornet killer' is. I believe nobody knows who she is, not even the ones who hire her. These men and women had lovers in the towns they visited. Now I need each assigned agent to get me a copy of the classifieds in the local newspaper in the towns where the victims lived. Find out what ads each victim's spouse ran in that paper. Then get the twenty papers before and after the date they were murdered. Contact us once you have all the papers."

Agent Sisson asked, "Aren't you going to tell us who did it?" He looked at Tender sharply.

"No. Not until I am a hundred percent sure," said Tender, shaking her head. Then she put her hand in mine. "Come on, Mom and Dad. Let's go home."

TWO

Mrs. Hines

The next day, David and I brought Tender to her Montessori school, as she was finally feeling better. Then we both went to police headquarters to work on a case. We received a case of a missing person; a thirty-six-year-old man who had gone missing ten days ago. We contacted the missing man's wife, Mrs. Kimberly Hines, for an interview. She agreed to meet us at 5 PM.

David and I picked Tender up at school at 4:30 PM, and then proceeded to Mrs. Hines' home. Mrs. Hines opened the door, and I was surprised that she was an older lady, in her mid-sixties. I wondered how she had come to be married to a thirty-six-year-old man.

As we introduced ourselves, I could see Mrs. Hines was taken aback that Tender was with us, two police officers. I explained to her that Tender was gifted and that she assisted the police on difficult cases. Even though Tender was only five, she was invaluable to us in solving our cases.

Then I turned the conversation to her missing husband. "Mrs. Hines, when was the last time you saw your husband?" I asked.

"Ten days ago," Mrs. Hines sniffled. She wiped her eyes with a handkerchief.

"What was the last thing you talked about?" I asked, taking notes in my notepad.

"We were planning a vacation to Florida," she answered, still sniffling.

Then Tender asked, "Mrs. Hines, how long have you lived here?"

"We moved here three years ago," Mrs. Hines replied. She couldn't help staring at Tender, curiously.

"Can we look around the house, Mrs. Hines? We may find a clue that will help us find your husband," I explained.

"Oh, yes, please do. I hope you can find something," Mrs. Hines said tearfully.

David stayed downstairs with Mrs. Hines, and Tender and I investigated around the house.

I whispered to Tender, "What does this mean? Her husband would be thirty years younger than her."

"Just follow me," Tender said. We went upstairs to the master bedroom, and Tender opened the bedroom closet. "See, Mom, no men's clothes."

"Do you mean there is no husband?" I asked, puzzled.

"No, but let's look in the other bedrooms. I noticed someone else had been living in there, most likely a man," Tender explained.

After we finished looking around the house, we went downstairs and told Mrs. Hines we would be back in a couple of days. She thanked us, and we left. There was nothing more we could do that day, but we decided tomorrow we would go to the post office and find out who had been living in that other bedroom.

David told us that when he was talking with Mrs. Hines, she was incredibly quiet, even though he tried to make conversation with her. By this time it was after 6 PM and we were all hungry, so we stopped at Ashlee's Pizzeria for dinner. After eating we went home and Tender wanted to read a book by herself.

I thought it would be better for us to have some fun together, so I said, "We are going to have a game night. Let's play Monopoly." The next few hours were about popcorn and family fun.

The next morning, after breakfast, we headed

to the post office. We discovered mail was being delivered to that address for a Victor Anderson. However, there was a forwarding address and service set up. We decided we would go to the address where the mail was being forwarded to as soon as we dropped Tender off at school. We proceeded to Victor's new location, about forty-five minutes away. We arrived just as he was leaving. We approached him, showing him our police badges. "Sir, are you Victor Anderson?" David inquired.

"Yes, officer, how can I help you?" he replied. "Only I'm on my way to work." He glanced at his watch.

"We just have a few questions; this won't take long. We are investigating a missing person," David explained.

"I am not sure I can help," Victor replied, glancing at his watch again.

"Do you know Mrs. Kimberly Hines?" David said. He looked steadily at Victor as he asked his question. I could tell he was working to keep the situation calm.

"Yes, I do. Is she all right?" Victor began to look concerned.

"Oh, yes. She reported her husband missing about ten days ago. Are you her husband?" David asked calmly.

Victor exhaled and shook his head. "I hate to tell you this, but she is not married. I used to rent a room from her, but I left ten days ago." His face had grown sad, and I noticed he had stopped looking at his watch.

"Can you tell us why you left?" I asked gently.

"I relocated to a new town when I got a new job. I loved living with Mrs. Hines, though. She would cook for me, do my laundry, iron my clothes—in fact, she treated me like I was her husband. But I drew the line when she wanted me to go out to dinner with her. I found a job forty-five minutes away, and it was too far to travel there and back each day. I am sorry, but I really must go now," said Victor, motioning toward his car.

We thanked him for his time and headed back to the station, very confused.

Back at the station, we went through the records of Mrs. Hines. We discovered she had been married, but her husband had died thirty years ago. We didn't know what to do.

As the afternoon was winding down, we picked up Tender from school and explained the situation about Mrs. Hines.

Tender felt that Mrs. Hines needed a friend. Perhaps if she had someone in her life, someone who was her friend, then she would be okay.

Tender said, "I have an idea. Let's go and see her again on Saturday."

"Tender, what do you have in mind?" I asked. I did not want her to make any promises to Mrs. Hines that she couldn't keep.

"You will see." said Tender with an extra cheerful grin.

For some reason, the week flew by. On Saturday, we still didn't know what Tender was planning.

Tender was so excited that she jumped into our bed bright and early Saturday morning.

"Tender Louise. It's Saturday; you know we sleep late." I groaned as her knee hit my stomach.

"I know that, of course, but it's time to get up. We have lots to do." Tender squealed and wiggled happily next to me in bed.

"I can't wait to see what she has in store ," said David, as he got up, brushed his teeth, and complained about being hungry.

I could hardly understand his mumbling with a toothbrush in his mouth, so I got up and made breakfast while David read his newspaper. Then we all got dressed and got ready to face the world.

"Okay, Dad. Take us to the animal shelter please," Tender directed.

"Aha, I think I see what you are up to," David smiled, swinging the car keys in his hand.

As we arrived, all we could hear were barking dogs. We entered, and Tender began chatting with the officer at the front desk right away. Tender explained our situation and that we needed a small dog with a pleasant personality. The dog would need to be trained already.

The animal control officer, Norman Carlson, knew us, as he was also part of a division of the police force.

"This is Skippy," he said as he introduced us to a small white dog with curly hair and a short tail that was wagging a hundred miles an hour. Skippy licked all our hands and barked happily. We knew immediately he was the right dog for the job. We signed the papers and listed Kimberly Hines as the new owner.

Back in the car, Tender said, "Mom and Dad, just go along with me, okay?"

David and I just looked at each other and shrugged. We arrived at Mrs. Hines' house and knocked on her door, with Skippy wiggling and wagging his tail. She was so pleased to see us, she never mentioned her missing husband.

Tender then told Mrs. Hines, "We have good news. We found Victor Anderson, and he said hi. He found a job and is doing well."

"Oh, thank you so much. That makes me feel

better," said Mrs. Hines. She gave Tender a big smile.

Tender continued, "Mrs. Hines, I have a problem. I found this cute dog Skippy at the city pound. I wanted to keep him, but we are too busy to have a dog. I was wondering if you could watch him for me. And I was hoping I would be allowed to come over and play with him sometimes."

Mrs. Hines took Skippy in her arms, and Skippy started licking her face. She laughed and said, "I would be happy to watch him for you." Skippy barked happily too. David had purchased dog food for Skippy to get him started. Tender said she wanted to stay the day with Mrs. Hines. Mrs. Hines was pleased with the idea of Tender's visit.

"Mom, Dad, pick me up at the end of the day, okay?" she grinned at us, while Skippy licked her hand.

I laughed and said, "Okay, darling. Mrs. Hines, is that all right with you?"

Mrs. Hines said she would be happy to have Tender stay and play with Skippy for the day. David and I were so excited to do whatever we pleased, alone for the day. We walked around a park, did some shopping, and ate lunch at a nice restaurant. The only problem was that before long, we missed Tender. At the end of the day, we picked her up, and I gave her a big hug and a kiss.

"I am so happy to see you, darling." I said.

"I was only away for a few hours, Mom," Tender laughed.

"Oh, I know. So how did it go?" I asked Tender.

"Excellent. Mrs. Hines loves Skippy. We took him for a walk, and then we played with him."

"What did you eat for lunch?" David asked, as always, thinking about food.

"Grilled cheese sandwiches," Tender replied.

"Mrs. Hines will be okay now, but we should check in on her soon to see how she and Skippy are doing," I said, smiling at her.

The next day, on Sunday, we decided to drop in on Mrs. Hines after church and invite her to lunch with us. She was so happy to be invited and gladly came along. She even brought Skippy.

Lunch that week was at David's parents, house, Jake and Louise (Grandpa and Grandma) Purdy. Skippy had fun playing with all the kids. From that day forward, we started picking up Mrs. Hines for church, and then she would come and enjoy a meal with us. She became like part of the family.

"I love it when we do what the Bible tells us to do—to treat our neighbors as ourselves," said Tender happily, as Skippy ran in circles around the backyard.

On Monday we took Tender to school, and David

and I headed to the police station. We met with Chief Purdy and briefed him on Mrs. Hines's missing person case.

"That sure was nice of Tender to help solve a simple case of kindness to Mrs. Hines," said Chief Purdy.

"Honestly, she always amazes us," David said with a laugh.

We chatted a little longer, and then Chief Purdy got down to business. "I heard from the FBI. They informed me they have the information that you requested on the 'hornet killer' case, he said. "It's important that you head over there to continue the case."

We gathered our things and headed over to Tender's school to pick her up. At the school, we spoke with Mrs. Adler, the principal, and apologized, since we had just dropped Tender off a short while ago. She always loved to hear the stories of Tender's cases after we had solved them. We informed her that this was an FBI case, and so far, very difficult.

When we arrived at headquarters, as usual, everyone waved to Tender and called out to say hi. At the front desk, Big John boomed out his big hello and handed Tender her rainbow lollipop. Big John used to be a top agent, but now that he was off active duty, he always staffed the front desk.

Every time Tender got a pop from Big John, David asked the same question: "Hey, what about me?" He would practically be drooling.

Big John would always give the same answer: "Agents only." Tender just looked at her dad and shrugged her shoulders.

Once we were upstairs, all the agents were eager to share what they had discovered. Agent Sisson explained, "This case just keeps getting stranger. All the partners of the victims posted the same ad in the 'help wanted' section. This is what the ad said: *'Wanted: help with the removal of a very large rodent. Please contact me at 455-555-1234.'*

"The phone number posted was different for each of the partners."

"Yes, but it was always placed from a home phone, and then another ad would be posted just days following the death of one of the victims. This classified ad was placed in the 'lost and found': *'I found a bag of money and would like to return it to the rightful owner. I placed it in a locker at the airport. Call me for the key only if you know the exact amount and color of the garment bag. Only then will I release the key.'* No phone number was posted, since the murderer already had the number." Agent Sisson reported.

Tender nodded and said, "Here is what happened

in every case. The spouse who was killed was having an affair, probably with their high school sweetheart or with someone they met while visiting relatives. They all used excuses to visit a family member back home. So, every month or so, they would say they needed to go home and visit. Most, if not all, had decided to leave their spouse and marry their lover." There was a murmur around the room as the agents considered this solution.

Agent Sisson asked, "How did the murderer get them to go home on a particular day?"

"That's easy; they all received a call that told them they could win a first-class ticket just by answering a question. It would be a simple question, like what is the closest planet to the sun?"

"Easy," Agent Sisson answered, "that's Mercury."

"Yes, that is correct. You have just won a first-class trip to any city in the U.S.," joked Tender. Another agent gave Agent Sisson a high-five and joked, "Way to go."

"I see now. So, the victims each thought they had won a free first-class ticket," Agent Sisson said, becoming serious again.

Tender went on. "I also noticed all the flights were on the same airline. The murderer is a stewardess. She is rather short, and had to be on every one of those flights."

Agent Sisson ordered the agents to look at the personnel who were assigned to these flights. "Tender, how is she getting first-class tickets to give away?" Agent Sisson asked.

"If you work for the airline, close relatives fly for free. She must have someone on the inside; she requests the ticket for a relative, and her partner makes sure no one checks up on it. This person, who is either her partner or her lover, is helping her for a cut of the money or for her attention," Tender explained.

Five days later, we received a call that the FBI had the 'hornet killer' and her accomplice in custody. She was an Asian stewardess who was trying to get $20,000 to get her husband and two children into the United States. Her accomplice spilled all the information after he found out that she was married and why she needed the money. He was also shocked to find out that after she was done with him, he would have been her last victim.

Two weeks later, we received the reward check for $5,000, from the FBI. The larger rewards come from private individuals or companies. As usual, David deposited the money in the account he had set up for Team Purdy.

THREE

Tender Loves Giving Gifts

One Sunday, during family lunch after church, Tender asked Grandpa Purdy if he could pick her up at school one day the next week at lunchtime. "I have something I need to take care of before Mom and Dad's anniversary next week," she explained.

Grandpa agreed, and they chose Wednesday at noon. She got permission from Mrs. Alder, since she let her in on what she had planned. "My Grandpa is picking me up to get a present for my parents' eighth wedding anniversary, which is May 25, 1965," Tender explained proudly.

Grandpa got there right at noon. Tender gave him a big hug, "I love you, Grandpa."

"I love you more!" he replied, squeezing her into a bear hug.

Tender gave him an even bigger smile.

"Where are we heading to?" Grandpa asked.

"Bismarck National Bank," Tender replied with a wink.

"Okay, I guess you need to get some money?" Grandpa asked.

"That's right," Tender nodded as she skipped to the car.

Once they arrived at the bank, the manager came over to greet them. "Good afternoon, Miss Tender, and Mr. Jake," he said courteously.

"Hi, Anthony," Grandpa answered. Grandpa always liked to be on a first-name basis with others.

"Follow me, please," said Mr. Ricci, as he escorted them to his office. He shuffled through papers on his desk. "Here are the papers you requested, Tender." Mr. Ricci handed a file of papers to Tender.

Tender looked them over carefully. Finally, she looked up and said she was satisfied.

Grandpa looked confused. "What's going on, Anthony?" he asked, raising his eyebrows.

"Oh, I'm sorry, Jake, I thought you knew. Tender is paying the balance of the mortgage on the property owned by your son, David, and his wife, Elaine."

Tears started to well up in Grandpa's eyes as Tender came over and gave him a kiss on his cheek. When the papers were presented to Grandpa, the balance was $11,620.86. He had to sign several documents.

Mr. Ricci also handed Tender an envelope with money in it. He then handed the discharge of mortgage document to Tender. He started to speak, but Tender cut in, "I know, I won't forget to go to city hall and record the discharge."

Mr. Ricci laughed. "You are a pretty smart little girl." he said, winking at Tender.

As they walked out together, Mr. Ricci whispered to Grandpa, "You know, she is one of the top 10 wealthiest depositors under 21 years old in our institution."

Grandpa replied, "I suspected she was."

After their trip to the bank, Grandpa and Tender went to her favorite restaurant for lunch. Grandpa enjoyed it too, as they served his favorite French fries. After lunch, they went to city hall to record the discharge of the mortgage. On their way back to Tender's school, Grandpa was curious about the envelope Mr. Ricci had handed to Tender.

"Grandpa, didn't you read all the papers you signed?" Tender asked, surprised.

"No. I assumed my attorney, Tender, knew what I was signing." They both laughed.

"Well, I can't tell you. It is a surprise, and you will see next week," Tender said mysteriously.

As Grandpa walked Tender into school, he kissed her on the cheek. "Tender, I love you," he said as he hugged her goodbye.

"Remember, Grandpa, mum's the word. And I love you too." Tender rejoined her class, and Grandpa went to the Bismarck Frame Company to have the recorded document installed in a glass frame.

Our anniversary was next Tuesday. We didn't know it, but there was going to be a surprise party after church on Sunday, at Grandpa and Grandma's house.

On Saturday, Tender woke up early again. She was excited because she and I were going shopping for my anniversary present for David. After our Saturday morning karate class, we freshened up and got ready to leave. David wanted us to take the '53 Corvette.

Tender was so excited, but I was terrified. I had driven it before, but it was always with David. I was always afraid I would put a dent in it. But today I was determined to conquer that fear.

So off we went, driving around in the Corvette looking for an anniversary present for David. The Corvette gives a bumpy ride, but we sure looked cool. "Tender, what do you think your father would like for our anniversary?" I asked, starting to relax behind the wheel.

"I know what he would like. A Craftsman riding lawnmower," Tender replied excitedly.

"Yes, you are right. I heard him complaining that soon he would have to start cutting the grass now that spring is here." I smiled happily, thinking of how surprised David would be. "Okay, then. Let's head to Sears," I said.

Once we arrived at Sears, we headed to the lawn and garden department. A Sears representative, William Anderson, came over. "Can I help you ladies find something?" he asked smoothly.

Tender spoke up. "We are looking for your Craftsman Heavy Duty garden tractor, with a 6-horsepower Lauzon engine. We would like the one with the 43-inch wheelbase."

William's jaw dropped. "Young lady, how did you know all that?"

"My dad receives your catalog in the mail," Tender replied. She fixed William with a no-nonsense stare.

"But how could such a young girl know all that information?" William stared at Tender in astonishment.

I spoke up. "Long story; don't ask."

William scratched his chin. "Well, that is our best model. It sells for $470."

"Tender, that is a lot of money," I hesitated. As

much as I wanted to give David the best anniversary present, I also didn't want to break our budget.

Tender reached into her purse, pulled out $235, and gave it to me. "I want to pay for half, Mom," she said. I bent down and gave her a hug right then and there.

Then I straightened up and looked at William. "We will take it." I said firmly.

"How wonderful ladies. So, when are you going to pick it up?" he asked.

Tender looked up. "Actually, sir, we know you are going to deliver it for free." she said smartly.

William looked taken aback, but he replied quickly, "I guess I am."

"We need it delivered on Tuesday," I explained.

William looked at the delivery schedule. "How about 11 AM?" he asked.

"That will be perfect. My grandpa will be there to receive it" Tender confirmed.

We paid in full and left the store like two giddy girls. "Your dad is going to love it. Thank you, Tender; I love you so much." Tender and I held hands as we walked to the car.

Later, we ate lunch at the Eveready Diner. We both had the special Big-D burger, fries, free drink, and ice cream shake.

After we got back home, I was ready for a nap.

Tender found David reading in the back yard. "Are you ready?" she asked him.

"You bet I am." David answered, jumping up. "Let's go!"

David decided to take the Corvette, too. "Okay, Tender, what did your mom get me for our anniversary?" he asked with a grin.

"She got you a nice tie," Tender replied, keeping a straight face, with her fingers crossed behind her back.

"What? A tie!" David exclaimed. Tender started to laugh.

"Come on, you can tell me. I promise I won't tell," David wheedled.

"Yes, I know you won't tell, because I am not telling you anything. I will give you a hint, though. You are going to love your present," Tender replied with a mysterious grin.

"Was it expensive?" David asked.

"Very expensive." Tender nodded.

"Okay, Tender, you win. Well, what should we get your mother?" he asked.

Tender said, "Either a new car, or a diamond necklace."

"Those are too expensive!" David spluttered.

"Don't worry about the cost; giving gifts is a good way to show your love," Tender replied, suddenly serious.

"Well, since you put it that way. Let's head over to Petersen Chevrolet," David said. As soon as they got there, a young salesman met them at the door.

"Good afternoon, folks; my name is Alex Petersen. How can I help you today?" he asked.

Tender spoke up. "We are looking for a new car for my mom."

David introduced himself, and then Alex took them to see one of the floor models.

"This one is . . ." Alex began to say.

Tender cut him off. "Stop!" she said, putting her hand up.

"My daughter would like to guess the car's features," David explained with a smile.

Alex looked surprised. "Okay, but I have never had anyone guess it right," he said with a shrug.

David replied, "Alex Petersen, I will bet you one free upgrade that she gets it 100 percent correct. How does that sound?"

"Wait here, and I will ask my dad" Alex went into the back room in a hurry.

Through the glass door, David and Tender heard him say, "Dad, I have a young girl who claims she can guess every item offered in one of our cars in the showroom." There was the sound of chairs being pushed back. Then Robert Petersen and several of the salesmen came out to see what was happening.

"Hi, Mr. Petersen, my name is Tender Purdy," said Tender calmly.

"How did you know me?" Robert asked, raising his eyebrows.

"That's easy; I noticed your name on your door," smiled Tender.

Robert chuckled. "Okay, Miss Tender, if you can guess everything offered in this car, I will give you one free upgrade. If not, you pay full price" He stuck out his hand, and Tender shook it.

Then Tender asked, "Could you open the hood?" David lifted her up, as she was too small to see inside.

"We have here a 1965 Chevelle Malibu Super Sport, two-door hardtop. The color is Regal Red, exterior and interior, with matching red carpets. It comes with a 396 V8 engine, with 350-horsepower, and a 4-barrel carburetor. It is the 300-body style with bucket seats. It comes with AM/FM radio, and four-on-the-floor standard transmission," Tender said, confidently listing off each detail.

David set her down and asked, "So, how did my little girl do?"

Robert shook his head in amazement. "I have never heard such a good description of any vehicle. Alex, I hope you were paying attention?"

"I sure was, Dad. That was interesting." Alex replied, as all the salesmen clapped their hands.

Tender asked, "Can we take it for a ride?"

"Yes. I will bring it outside for you," Alex replied eagerly, as he closed the hood and polished it up.

"Before we do that, what is the price?" David asked anxiously.

"Only $2,796," Alex replied.

David pulled Tender to one side. "Honey, we can't afford this." he said sadly.

"Dad, can you come up with $796?" Tender asked, looking him straight in the eyes.

"Yes, I could pay that much." David agreed.

"Then let's take it for a ride," Tender said, patting him on the arm.

As they drove down the road, David looked over at Tender. "Your mom will love this car, Tender. It has lots of power."

"You're right, Dad. Let's take it." Tender replied, rolling down the window and feeling the wind in her hair.

"Well, you must know something I don't know, I don't have the money to buy any car, never mind this one, Tender." David said as he turned the car back toward the dealership.

In the parking lot, Tender slipped an envelope into David's hand.

"Tender, what's this? Where did you get all this money?" David asked in shock.

"It's mine, Dad. It's part of the money we earned for the 'Hornet Killer' case. But I'm giving it to you to buy Mom's gift." Tender said, smiling sweetly at her dad.

David couldn't speak for a minute. Then finally he hugged Tender close and whispered, "Thank you, honey."

As they walked back in, Alex greeted them eagerly. "So how was the test ride? Are you ready to buy?"

"Just a minute. What about our free upgrade?" demanded Tender. She wasn't going to forget.

Alex handed the list of upgrades over to her. Tender looked it over, but then she gave it to David. "Dad, you choose," she said.

David decided to go with the undercoating, which would protect the bottom of the car from rusting. He sat down and signed the paperwork and informed Alex that he wanted a temporary twenty-one-day license plate. He also requested Alex to have it ready for Tuesday.

Alex promised it would be ready. Then Tender and David walked back out to the car.

David was still processing everything that had happened. "Tender, you are so generous to your mom and me. I love you, honey," he said, choking up a little.

"I love you very much, Dad. But I know you did this so that Mom and I will look cool driving down the road," Tender teased. David laughed so hard, he had to wipe his eyes.

Back at home, I kept trying to trick Tender into telling me what David had bought for me. Tender said, with her fingers crossed behind her back again, "He bought you chocolates and flowers."

I gave David a dirty look.

"What?!" he yelped.

"You better not have gotten me just flowers and chocolates after what I bought for you." I said, with my eyes narrowed.

David looked at Tender. "I guess we better go out again and buy something else." David teased.

"Not tonight, Dad. I am tired," said Tender with a big yawn. Then they both looked at each other and burst out laughing.

Sunday morning arrived. It always seemed to be the most chaotic day of the week, with everyone getting ready at the same time. As soon as we were all dressed for church, we were off to pick up Mrs. Hines and Skippy. The whole family was glad to see them. She was surprised at how much food we ordered at the Eveready Diner for breakfast. After breakfast, it was off to church.

Mrs. Hines was so thankful to be joining her

"new family" every Sunday. Tender told her about the surprise party today for our eighth anniversary. She also asked her to make up an excuse to visit the local convenience store after church before going to Grandpa and Grandma's house. I wondered what she had in mind.

After the church service, Mrs. Hines asked David if they could stop off at the store first. Tender went in with her, and they spent a long time purchasing a small gift that would fit in her purse. Finally, we were on our way to Grandma and Grandpa's home. Everyone who wasn't a Sunday regular parked their cars in the neighbors' driveways. Since all the neighbors were invited, they didn't mind. As we all entered the home, Grandma welcomed us and told us everyone was in the backyard.

David and I were shocked when the crowd yelled, "SURPRISE!" Everyone had a glass and a knife in their hands and started tapping them together. David and I laughed and kissed, and then I hugged Tender. We both bent down, kissed her, and told her we loved her.

"Mom, I am so happy to be a Purdy," sighed Tender happily.

Everyone who had been invited was there, even our old college friends. Linda and Roger came, along with their two boys, Roger Jr. and Peter. Joann and Michael came with their little girl, Emily.

Tender and Skippy were having a great time entertaining little Emily. The party was so much fun; the Purdys have a special gift for entertaining guests. After everyone finished their meals, we had cake and ice cream. Then David and I sat in the center and started to open the gifts. I did not want to show all the gifts we received; I just thanked the giver and kept the gift in the box.

Finally, Grandpa brought out a gift from Tender. Grandpa asked us to read the card first. It read:

Dear Mom and Dad, I could never have imagined being in such a loving family. It reminds me that when I accepted Jesus as my Savior, I was adopted unconditionally into the family of God. Thank you for saving me from life in an orphanage. I love you both too much for words. Tender Louise.

David and I opened the package and looked at the glass frame. When we saw what it was, I started to sob, and even David had tears in his eyes.

Everyone wanted to know what it was, so I turned the picture frame around to reveal the house mortgage paid in full. Everyone sighed and took a deep breath.

I put my arms out, and Tender ran over and jumped into my arms. David also joined in, and we both told her we loved her very much. I whispered into her ear, "Tender, I feel like I have been your mother all your life."

"I feel the same way, Mom and Dad. I love you," Tender smiled. There were tears in her eyes too.

After the gifts, people started to leave. We left too, thanking Grandma and Grandpa for a fun party. On the way home, I could not hold it in any longer; I had to talk to Tender about her gift to us.

"Tender, it was Dad's and my responsibility to pay off the mortgage, not yours," I said, gently but firmly.

"Mom and Dad, I thought long and hard before I decided to go ahead and do that. I came up with two reasons why I should do it. First, when you pass away, I believe you will leave this house and all your property to me." Tender said, raising up one finger.

David said, "We have already made out a will, and you will inherit everything we own. We have also assigned guardianship."

"Really? Who did you choose?" asked Tender curiously.

I asked Tender with a smile, "Who would you prefer as your guardian?"

"My Aunt Mary" Tender exclaimed right away.

"Good. That's who we chose. We have asked

her if she would take the responsibility of being your guardian if we were both to pass away," I said, smiling even more.

"Okay, Tender, what was the second reason?" asked David.

"The second reason is that when we go on a case, we are a team, and if we get a reward, it belongs to all of us, not just me," said Tender, holding up a second finger.

As we pulled into the garage, David asked Tender to get the mail. Once we were in the house, Tender handed it to him. He always goes over to his lounge chair and opens his mail. There were several anniversary cards, which he put aside for me to open. Then he noticed a letter that seemed heavy and had no stamp. Surprised, he called the family over to the kitchen table.

"This is strange; we received a suspicious letter with no postage," David said.

Tender and I looked it over and noticed there was also no return address. Detective Tender noted that it was a business-size envelope.

We knew that when a suspicious letter arrived, we needed to call Chief Purdy right away. Chief Purdy decided to send over the hazmat unit to our house. Chief Purdy arrived first, and then the hazmat team showed up not too long afterward.

They put the envelope safely in a bomb-proof container. Then we all headed to police headquarters, where they checked the package for fingerprints. There were three sets: most likely Tender's, David's, and those of the mailman. The letter was placed in a bulletproof plexiglass enclosure, which had rubber holes installed so both hands would fix tight keeping any toxic chemicals from escaping. Before the hazmat officer opened the envelope, everyone had to station themselves to watch from the observation room. Using special tongs and dressed in a hazmat suit, the officer opened the envelope. He handled the package delicately as we observed and listened to his step-by-step explanation of what he witnessed. He opened the envelope, and it had no sign of any chemical or powder. Finally, he removed the letter from the envelope, opened it, and held it up. We could see it was done in headline graphics, glued to a plain piece of paper.

"Someone has cut out letters from another source and pasted them onto this piece of paper," observed Tender.

"That's how most ransom notes are written," I commented with a frown.

Tender replied, "They are easy to investigate, because the author usually makes too many mistakes."

Chief Purdy asked us to go home. They took a Polaroid photo of the letter and gave it to David. Then Chief Purdy said, "Call me in the morning and we will discuss our options."

Once back home, we gathered around the kitchen table.

David looked at the picture of the letter for a few minutes and then said, "I can't tell what they are saying." He threw his arms in the air in frustration.

Tender took the letter and studied it for about ten minutes. I looked over her shoulder. All I could see was nonsense:

eidronwotevaeltsriflrigehtemdesuacuoymrahe-htrofuoyhtiwnevetegotgniogmalsesacesehtlla-gnivlostatramserauoyknihtuoysydrupolleh

Tender asked me, "Please get a paper, and write what I tell you." I quickly got a piece of notepaper and a pencil. Tender dictated:

Hello Purdy's, you think you are smart at solving all these cases. I am going to get even with you for the harm you caused me. The girl first. Leave town or die.

FOUR

Protective Custody

I gasped, and my hands shook. "Tender, what do you think? Are you in danger?" I asked.

"No, Mom. This is just a diversion, a scare tactic to get us to leave town," Tender replied reassuringly. She put her hand on mine to stop them from shaking.

"How do you know that?" I asked, unsure.

"If someone wanted to murder us, they would want us to stay in town, not leave. And they would never have given us a warning." Tender observed calmly.

David replied, "That makes sense." He could see I was upset though, so he moved over and put his arm around me.

"If I intended to kill someone, I would never tell two detectives who carry a gun every place they go. I would plan a surprise attack for when they least expected it." Tender said. She gave my hands a squeeze.

"I suppose you are right. I feel better, but don't go anywhere without us until this case is solved," I said, trying to keep my voice from trembling.

"Okay, Mom," Tender replied seriously.

"Starting tonight, you sleep in our bed with me. David, you'll have to sleep on the couch," I instructed.

"Yes, ma'am!" David saluted me. I gave him a weak smile.

"Tender, what do you think they are up to?" I said, as we snuggled together in bed.

"I am not sure, Mom. But it will be big." Tender yawned and was fast asleep in minutes. I barely slept a wink all night.

Nothing happened during the night, and the next morning we informed Mrs. Adler that Tender was under protective custody and would not be in school until further notice. Tender was not concerned, because she knew David and I would never let her out of our sight. As we left the house, we put three suitcases, with enough clothes to last a few days into the trunk of our car, just in case we were being watched, to make it look like we were leaving town.

We made our way to FBI headquarters, where

Agent Sisson invited Chief Purdy to be on the task force.

Tender started to explain her point of view about what the note said and why she was not in any danger. She explained that instead of a murder, we needed to be ready to stop a robbery.

Agent Sisson asked, "A robbery? What is going to be robbed?" He looked from Tender to David to me in confusion.

Tender said, "I don't believe it will be a bank, because banks take too long, and they could only get a few thousand from the tellers drawer. Then there is the problem of getting out of town during daylight. It also won't be an armored car, because those are easy to spot, and the drivers and the security personnel are all armed.

"So, what you're saying is, you have no idea," replied Agent Sisson, looking frustrated. He slapped his palms down on the table.

Tender just smiled. "No, that is not what I am saying. Let me ask you all a question: On Sunday where would you find the largest amount of money?" No one could answer. Then finally David exclaimed, "The horse racetrack!"

Tender nodded, "Yes. They are most likely going to rob the North Dakota Horse Park. It is located near two major roads, which makes for an easy getaway. First, it is loud when a race starts. Second, it is off the beaten path and not found anywhere near the Fargo police station. Third, there is always lots of money upstairs after each race until all the money is moved. Fourth, the security is supplied by a private contractor, which will be replaced by a fake security force. Fifth, one or two of the real security force personnel are involved. A company armored vehicle will show up to collect the money, but then it will be replaced a few miles down the road. The company doing security is the Bismarck Security Force. First, you will need to locate the unmarked car that will be hidden along the getaway route by Saturday. The rest is up to you to decide how to proceed." Tender sat down and looked up at Agent Sisson, motioning for him to take over.

Agent Sisson, Chief Purdy, David, and all the agents stayed behind waiting for their assignments, as this would take a lot of coordination. Meanwhile, Tender and I left to go to lunch in the FBI cafeteria.

Agent Sisson was in charge, and he had the Fargo police force double their on-duty officers on Saturday and Sunday. They needed to be on the lookout for a car, possibly a station wagon in the surrounding area close too major roads. They were also asked to search all the dirt roads within one mile of the track.

Agent Sisson called a meeting early Saturday morning. First, he named the operation 'Seabiscuit'. He instructed all the agents to be careful while inside the track. Agents were also instructed to allow the money to be taken. Once they confirmed the criminals had the cash, they would report it on the FBI radio frequency. There would be many police officers, from Bismarck and Fargo, along with ten FBI agents with unmarked vehicles ready to pursue the criminals.

Agent Sisson summarized the operation: "Here is how we predict it will go. The criminals will be thinking that they have gotten away with the robbery. So, once they approach the station wagon, they will load it before starting it. However, we will have found and disabled the vehicle. Once they realize they can't start it, they will load the money back into the security van. That's when we move in. Let's watch each other's backs and all come home safe."

Late Saturday morning, the station wagon was located in a wooded area with tree branches on the roof. The police picked up the local mechanic who repairs all the police vehicles and brought him in an unmarked vehicle to where the station wagon was hidden. He disabled the vehicle by removing the cable to the starter, a part that the criminals would not be able to replace during their getaway.

Sunday morning arrived. The first race started at 10 AM. All was going as planned. The last race was at noon, and at 12:30 we all heard, "'Seabiscuit' is on the move," coming over the FBI scanners. Unmarked vehicles followed the fake security vehicle, turning off every few miles to be replaced with a different unmarked vehicle, to keep the criminals from becoming suspicious.

Agent Sisson bellowed into his scanner, "Tree Huggers Unit, Seabiscuit heading your way!" As the criminals got out of the security vehicle and approached the station wagon, they all started slapping one another on the back, shouting, and jumping for joy. They started to load the money into the waiting wagon. They all piled in with ten bags of money and tried to start it. However, the wagon wouldn't start. After several failed attempts, they realized they needed to put the money back in the van. Now time would be against them.

Then, over a loudspeaker, they heard, "This is the FBI! We have you surrounded. Put your hands up in the air, then lie face down on the ground with your hands behind your neck." All the criminals were so shocked that they all complied and did as they were told.

Tender and I stayed at home, under police protection, during the FBI operation to keep her safe.

We both sat by the phone, waiting for a call from David. We did not have to wait long, he called and then soon came home. We were so happy that he was safe. Even though it was a good plan, we both knew that sometimes plans do not work out.

David sat down and explained how the operation went down, with no one getting hurt. "Tender, you were correct; there were two inside helpers and five other suspects," he said, taking a long drink of water. It had been a long day in the field.

"My only regret," Tender remarked, "is that we missed church and couldn't spend time with family and friends." David had warned our family, friends, and even Pastor Bob from church that they should be careful or even stay home.

On Monday at 10 AM, we were to report to Director Lance at the FBI. David was all keyed up before we left so he went for a jog. We arrived early for the meeting, so with Tender's pass we planned to enjoy a free breakfast at the FBI cafeteria. Tender sure enjoyed having all the FBI privileges.

When we entered FBI headquarters, Big John called over to Tender. "Aren't you going to say hi?" he said in his big, booming voice.

"Good morning, Big John." Tender grinned and gave him a high-five.

"So, Tender, did you do it again with the 'Seabiscuit' case?" Big John winked at her.

Tender only smiled and took the giant lollipop he was holding out to her. Then David put his hand out too.

"Agents only." growled Big John. Then he called after us, "I love that girl." David and I laughed and waved to Big John. He waved back.

After our breakfast, we took the elevator upstairs. As we entered the investigation room all the agents clapped for Tender.

Director Lance announced, "Congratulations to everyone who helped us stop a major crime with no one getting injured, or worse. It's all thanks to Agent Sisson who proved, again, he understands how to handle dangerous situations. Tender, come up here please."

Tender walked to the front of the room. Director Lance put his hand on her shoulder. "This girl has an ability to see problems differently than anyone else I know. She solved another case and saved the North Dakota Horse Park over fifty thousand dollars. I hereby present you with a check from them, along with this note."

Thank you so much and keep up the good work. Thank you for stopping the robbery of the North Dakota Horse Park. Signed, Robert Chester, Chairman of the board.

Everyone clapped again and cheered for Tender.

They had all come to love her and see the way she solved the most difficult cases.

Afterward, Director Lance asked to see us in his office. We all went in and sat down in front of his desk.

"Congratulations, Purdys. Wonderful job; you are all amazing. Well, that's another case solved." Director Lance smiled.

"The only one we haven't solved yet is what happened to Vicky Smith," I said, glancing over at Tender.

"I'm sorry to say that's true; we still don't know where she is. But for now, Chief Purdy would like you to report to him," Director Lance said, ushering us out the door.

As we headed over to police headquarters, Tender did not say a word. I could tell she was upset; I could even hear her sniffling a little in the back seat.

When we arrived at the police station, Chief Purdy greeted us and explained that he had a new cold case for us.

"This case involved a hit-and-run, resulting in death. These are the most difficult cases. The accident happened late one night, three years ago on a country road. Because of pressure from the family and from council member Jack Evans, I have decided to reopen the case," said Chief Purdy, handing the case file to David.

Because Tender was still upset, I decided to wait to talk about the new case until she was feeling better. For some reason I couldn't understand, why she was more concerned about Vicky Smith than this case.

David went to pick up Mary and Richard as they were walking from school toward our house.

"David, we have some good news." blurted out Richard as soon as they arrived. "Mary and I want to tell you everything we learned." However, before they could say anything else, David handed Richard and Mary a check for their share of the cases we just solved. Richard and Mary looked wide-eyed at the check, then at David.

Tender laughed and explained about the robbery and 'hornet killer' cases. She told about receiving reward checks for both solved cases. Mary and Richard just stared at her.

"I do not understand. You received that much reward money for two cases?" asked Mary incredulously. Richard just stood there gaping.

"Yes, sometimes when we help the FBI, Team Purdy receives a reward, sometimes we receive more from private cases." I smiled and put my hand on Mary's shoulder.

Richard still had his mouth open, so Mary poked him, calling him back down to earth. Tender laughed out loud at their amazed expressions.

"Okay, I need to know what you discovered about Vicky Smith, the only girl still missing." Tender said, becoming serious.

"We think we have found where she is. We contacted, many deaf schools, and the only one we found suspicious was in Texas. They would not answer any of our questions. It is hidden away, almost ten miles from the nearest house," Richard reported, still looking in awe at the check.

Mary grabbed the check from Richard, and he fell back against the cushions of his chair and let out a long breath. Then he ruffled his hair with his hand and grinned at Mary.

Mary continued with their story. "I contacted the local sheriff and his deputy, and they are both concerned about what goes on out there. It is an all-deaf commune."

Tender stood up and began pacing around the room. "Dad, since the FBI closed the case, what can we do?"

"Without their help, we will not be able to move forward with the case," he said, looking at Tender sadly. He tried to give her a hug, but she kept on pacing.

"Tomorrow, we will go to Director Lance and insist he reopen the case," Tender said, suddenly stopping and stamping her foot.

Then David surprised Mary and Richard by taking their check and having them both endorse it. He explained, "I will open an account in all our names: me, you and Richard. If at any time you want or need any funds, just ask, and I will give you a check out of your account. I will also pay you the hourly wages once a case is complete."

We spent a pleasant evening listening to Richard and Mary tell us all about the wonderful school leaders they spoke to. The next day Tender went to school and David and I went to work on our cold case.

We put in a call to Agent Sisson, asking to meet with Director Lance, but we only got his answering machine. About midday, we got a phone call back from Agent Sisson, letting us know we could stop by to see Director Lance after Tender's school day ended.

As we entered FBI headquarters Big John came over to Tender and thanked her for saving the 59 missing girls, in the case of the 60 missing girls.

"No, thank you for keeping me safe. I love you," Tender smiled.

Big John gave Tender her rainbow pop, as usual.

Then David put his hand out. "Remember, you promised once we found the girls, I would get a pop too." David's eyes were wide open, and he was almost drooling. Big John playfully slapped his hand.

"So, are you saying you have recovered all sixty girls?" he said in his big booming voice.

I grabbed David's arm and said, "Watch yourself, now! You can't trick John Riley."

David rubbed his arm. "Hey, that hurt." he exclaimed. We all laughed.

"Tender, anytime you need help, I would love to be on your team. I love you, girl," Big John said, looking straight at Tender. "You can count on me." Tender thanked him, and then we went upstairs to see Director Lance. We had to wait for over an hour.

When we finally got in to see Director Lance, he greeted us with his usual pleasantries "Hello Purdys, how nice to see you. You did such a great job saving those fifty-nine girls last month. You are the talk of the country, and the Secretary of the Navy wanted me to thank you personally." Director Lance gave a brief smile. "So, how can I help you?" he asked.

I explained all the evidence we had discovered, but Director Lance shook his head.

"You don't have enough evidence to warrant a search of their property," the director said shortly.

We were baffled by his denial, and I was surprised at how angry Tender got. She started to walk out without us. Then she turned around and said, "Two can play this game."

Director Lance got angry. "What does she mean? Doesn't she know who I am?" he growled.

"I guess not, and you will find out," David said, shrugging his shoulders and looking defiantly at Director Lance.

"Tender, what are you going to do?" I asked, concerned. As we went downstairs, Tender would not answer me. With a stern face, she walked very quickly through the lobby. "Tender, slow down!" I called, but she wouldn't stop Instead, she marched over to the front desk and handed Big John her FBI badge.

"Tender, what is this?" Big John boomed out.

"I am no longer an agent with the FBI." She stomped her foot and stormed out.

Big John turned to us. "What happened?" I followed after Tender, and David explained the situation to Big John.

Big John was so angry when he heard what happened that he took Tender's badge and marched right up to Director Lance's office.

On the way home we picked up pizza. Tender reminded us, "Don't forget to get one for Mary and

Richard and bring an extra-large with cheese only."
Once again, Mary and Richard were waiting for us,
expecting to hear good news. We had to break it to
them what had happened.

"I can't believe it! After all you have done for
the FBI, they would not even investigate the case,"
exclaimed Mary. After about ten minutes, we heard
a loud knock at the door. Richard went over to
answer it. As he opened it, he jumped back, "Big
John you scared me.

"Can I help you?" Richard said nervously.

"Yes, I want to talk to Tender," came a big booming voice. Tender knew that voice right away, and
she came over to Big John and gave him a hug.
David and I followed.

"Is Director Lance going to investigate this
Texas case?" Tender asked.

"No. He said he is not going to put any more
agents on this case." Big John stomped his foot and
folded his arms. "I also got suspended for getting
angry and saying some things I shouldn't have. I
gave him your badge on my way out," Big John said.
Then he glanced at Tender and said, "He thinks
you will be fine in a few days."

Tender replied, "I will not be fine until Vicky is
home." She set her jaw stubbornly.

Big John joined us for pizza; Tender had

requested the extra-large cheese pizza for him. Once everyone was served, Big John asked to be introduced to Mary and Richard. As Richard shook his head, all he could say was, "Sir, you sure gave me a scare when I opened the door." Big John just chuckled and slapped Richard on the back.

David explained to Big John about Tender's concern for Vicky. "For some reason, Tender needs to find this deaf girl, Vicky, more than the other fifty-nine that were found," David said as he helped himself to another slice of pizza.

"Big John, do you know the Bible story about the Good Shepherd?" I asked.

"No," Big John answered, turning to listen.

"The Bible says that the Good Shepherd, who is Jesus, left the ninety-nine sheep that were safely in the fold to search for the one lost sheep. That's how Tender feels about the one lost girl," I explained, pouring myself a glass of water.

"I understand why Tender needs to find the lost girl, but what reason did the director give for denying Tender?" Big John asked, furrowing his brows.

"He did not feel it worth risking more agents on one lost runaway." Tender said, very angrily.

"Tender, FBI policy states that once they have had a success rate over 90 percent, they believe the chances of getting the last 10 percent are like finding a needle in a haystack—impossible odds," replied Big John sadly.

"I cannot give up. I must find her." Tender started crying.

Big John picked her up and held her so gently for a big man. All the while, Tender cried, he never said a word. Everyone kept quiet until Tender calmed down.

Finally, Tender wiped her eyes and said, "Dad, I looked over your unsolved case in order to get my mind off of Vicky."

"Okay, honey," he said. "Let's head into the investigation room."

"Big John, would you like to sit in;" I offered.

"Yes, please. I would love to see Tender at work. Also, I am suspended until further notice, and without pay," Big John said wryly.

We entered the room, and David began to explain the case, which he loved to do. "This is what we have so far: On February 16, 1962, on a Friday night, a red car, traveling too fast hit a 1957 Chevy Nomad carrying Alice McCoy and her daughter, Connie. They were just returning from Alice's mother's fiftieth birthday party, where no alcohol was served, making it a dry party."

"So, Alice was not intoxicated while driving," Big John confirmed.

"Alice left the party at approximately 11 PM However, they never made it home. They were reported missing, and they were both discovered a week later, about ten minutes from her mother's house, on a winding road with a twenty-foot-deep embankment. They did not die for several days," David reported.

"Wait, so if the driver who had caused the accident had only stopped, they would have both survived." exclaimed Richard.

"That we will never know. Even if he had stopped, they both might still have died," I pointed out.

"Usually, a person with serious injuries from such a long fall is unlikely to survive," Tender replied.

"Alice's car, the Nomad, was stolen a few months ago from the impound yard, so, under a lot of pressure, Chief Purdy reopened this cold case," David said.

"Why was it assigned to you? " Big John asked.

"David is the head of the cold case unit. We are given all the cold cases. Tender sees these cases differently than everyone else on the police force. Chief Purdy wants the person arrested and charged. It is one of the few cases for which our city is offering a reward to the person who brings forward enough information leading to an arrest and conviction," I said.

Big John asked, "Do you have any clues?" He twirled his pencil over his notepad.

"Has Tender looked over the case?" Mary wanted to know.

"Yes, I first looked at all the photos for the crime scene, looking for the paint color that was transferred onto vehicle number one from vehicle number two." Tender reported.

"Which one is vehicle two?" asked Richard.

"Vehicle number one is the victims vehicle, and vehicle number two was driven by the person who caused the accident," replied David.

"This is what I have observed: vehicle two hit vehicle one. The paint color that transferred from vehicle two to vehicle one was Matador Red. Due to the picture fading I believe that's the color, which was made by Dupont in 1958 and was used on the 1958 Corvette. Using my magnifying glass and making my best guess, the color seems to be from a 1958 Corvette. I believe this car was sold not too long after the accident." Tender said.

"Tomorrow I will head to police headquarters and explain what we have discovered." David said excitedly.

"Mary and Richard, you will head to the *Bismarck Daily News* archives and look through the classified ads starting with February 16, 1962, the day the accident occurred, until you find any ads for 1958 Corvettes offered for sale during the year of 1962, no matter the color." David said.

"Is there anything Tender doesn't know?" asked Big John with a chuckle.

"Not much," answered David, chuckling too.

"Tender, who are you more like, your mom or your dad?" Big John asked.

"Both." Tender replied. David and I looked at each other, and at the same time, we said, "I agree." Then we all laughed.

The next day, David and I took Tender to school, and then went to work.

Chief Purdy was excited about what Tender had discovered. He wondered if Tender could stop by after school so he could talk to her. Once she arrived, he stood and thanked her and asked if she wanted to lead the investigation.

"No, sir. I would love for my dad and mom to lead this investigation with the police force," Tender said as she smiled up at Chief Purdy.

"Very well. Then your dad and mom will lead." asked Chief Purdy, nodding to us.

"I would be honored, sir," said David. "I always follow you ladies anyway," he said with a wink my way.

"Then it's settled. In the morning, I will have

a team ready to start the investigation." ordered Chief Purdy.

That evening, Richard, Mary, and Big John came over to share the evidence they had found. David brought home pizza for dinner.

Richard, Mary, and Big John were all excited to get into the investigation room, but I insisted we eat our pizza in the kitchen. While we were eating, Tender asked, "So, how did you three do today?"

"How do you know we were working together?" asked Big John.

"I can tell you more if you like." she smiled.

"Yes, give it a try," Big John said, laughing.

"Mary and Richard skipped school today because it is national skip day for seniors. Big John was at the Bismarck local news office at 7:30 AM, a half-hour early, but Richard and Mary got there at 8:15 AM, after breakfast. Richard's mother thought it important he skip school today because she believes in school traditions. On the other hand, my grandpa is going to ground Mary for a week. The three of you worked great as a team, sharing ideas. And now for the rest, wait until we enter the investigation room." Tender smiled as Big John just shook his head in wonder. The rest of us were never in doubt that she would get all the details correct.

Finally, we finished eating, cleaned up, and went into our home investigation room. Richard stood and gave the report.

"During the time from February 16, 1962, to April 30, 1962, we discovered sixteen Corvettes for sale. To our surprise, six were painted assorted colors from that year."

"So, what do we do now?" Mary asked.

"Mary, you and Richard will call the past owners of the six cars, and follow my directions," Tender said. "First, introduce yourselves by giving them a phony name. Ask them for their name, but do not push it. Remember, you might be talking to a murderer. Tell them you are interested in finding a 1958 Corvette. Explain that your father passed away and you are trying to track down his 1958 Corvette, and you are willing to pay $2,500. Once you explain all that, ask if the Corvette they owned had ever been in an accident."

"Wait. If we ask that, and they did have an accident, they will hang up!" Richard exclaimed.

"That's what we want. If they do that, then they might be the person we are looking for." explained Tender. "If they keep talking, then the next question you ask is what color it was when they sold it, and did they have it painted. Finally, ask them if they remember who they sold it to. Thank them for all their help, and hang up before they can ask you any questions."

Mary and Richard had been writing down all of Tender's instructions. When Tender was sure they understood everything, she said, "Big John, you go with them and listen in. See if anyone acts nervous over the questions," Tender directed.

"Will do, boss," Big John agreed as the three of them started out to the kitchen to make calls right away.

After an hour, they reported back. "Well, four out of the six possible suspects answered the phone. However, one didn't want to answer any questions, and seemed very nervous," offered Big John.

"Mary, tell us exactly what was said," instructed David.

"The three that answered questions all answered almost identically. They all had to have their cars painted, as the color had faded. None were Matador Red to start with, but one was painted Matador Red. None had been in an accident, that they knew of. They all gave me their names and the name of the person they sold the car to. Some even asked if I wanted to see if the owners wanted to sell. At that time, I hung up," Mary reported.

Tender put her hands over her face. I noticed she was doing that much more often.

"Tender, darling, is everything all right?" I asked, concerned.

"Yes, Mom," Tender replied, not taking her hands off her face.

"Tender, why are you putting your hands over your face?" I inquired.

"I have to be able to see the problem live," Tender said, her voice muffled by her hands.

"Tender, what do you see?" asked Richard eagerly. I gave him a reproachful look.

"I see a good man making a mistake and living with the guilt that a mother and daughter are dead because he was drunk." Tender took her hands off her face and stood up.

"Big John, tomorrow I want you to go to the Registry of Motor Vehicles and find out who purchased and registered a 1958 Corvette from February 16 to April 30 of the same year," Tender said.

Big John slapped his hand on the table and said, "Right." Then he looked confused. "How will I know the right car? I do not know the owner's name or the buyer's name," Big John questioned.

"First, go to the *Bismarck Daily News*, and find the dates that the ad ran. It would be for no more than a week. Then go to the Registry of Motor Vehicles and find every 1958 Corvette that transferred a title during that time period. From there you might have to show your FBI badge to get access to the original owner," David said.

"Well, it is past our bedtime. Mary and Richard, I will drive you home," David said with a yawn.

"Thank you, all. I am so enjoying this time together," Big John said as he got up and stretched.

Tender went over and hugged everyone good night. "We couldn't have gotten so much done without your help, Big John," she said with a smile.

David was getting ready to leave with Richard and Mary, but he waited until Big John was ready to leave.

"Big John, I love you the most of any non-family member," Tender said as she hugged him.

"Big John, please join us Sunday for church, or at least for lunch. We always gather for lunch as a family after church," I invited him with a smile.

"I would love to. What church, and what time?" Big John asked as he put on his shoes.

"Service at Bismarck Christian Church is at 11 A.M., and we all meet for breakfast at 9 A.M. at the Eveready Diner," I explained.

Big John wrote down the information and promised he would see us there. After Big John left, David asked all of us to meet. in the living room to discuss what was on his mind.

"We need to vote on whether to invite Big John

to be a team member full time. Any questions?" David said as we all sat down.

Mary raised her hand, "How do these meetings work? This is the first meeting for Richard and me," she inquired.

"I am the only member who can request a meeting and the only one who can propose adding to the team," David informed them.

"Why only you?" Richard asked, leaning forward.

"It can become too confusing if we have too many different ideas. This way, you either vote thumbs-up or thumbs-down. Do you know who decided to have Tender leave the FBI?" David continued.

"Tender," Richard and Mary said together.

"Actually, we all did. We would never let one team member go it alone. If the director denied our request to investigate at least the possibility of a crime being committed, Tender was to resign. And unless he changes his mind, we are standing strong," David said firmly.

Mary and Richard nodded seriously.

"Okay, time to vote." David said briskly.

"Tender?" Tender gave a thumbs-up.

"Elaine?" I gave a thumb-up too.

"Mary?" Mary gave a thumbs-up.

"Richard?" Richard gave a thumbs-up too.

"Hey, can I change my name to be a Purdy?"

Richard said. Everyone laughed and then put their thumbs down.

"Richard, I think Mary is looking forward to being Mary Harris," Tender replied with a smile.

"Tender, I haven't even been asked yet," Mary replied, blushing. Everyone stared at Richard to see how he would respond.

"I will only say this about getting married: Mary is going to have to wait until I graduate from the criminal justice program at Bismarck State College." Next thing he knew, Mary had jumped into his lap and was hugging him.

"I love you, Richard Paul Harris." Mary squealed.

"Not as much as I love you, Mary Ann Purdy," Richard said, hugging her back.

"Okay, let's get you two home," David demanded.

They left, and I put Tender to bed. We read a book, and then I kissed her good night.

Meanwhile, David dropped off Richard. Mary turned to David, and asked, "So why is it so import- ant to wait until after college to get married?"

"Mary, Mom and Dad don't believe in long engagements, so you will need to ask them first," said David as he dropped her off. Mary kissed her brother on the cheek and told him she loved our family very much.

"I still don't know what Elaine sees in you." Mary laughed.

"I could say the same thing about you, Mary. " David exclaimed.

"Oh, no, you can't." she fired back.

"You are right. All the women in this family are more intelligent than the men," David conceded. They both laughed and said goodnight.

Once David was back home, I informed him that his cousin, Loriann, had left a message on the answering machine.

FIVE

Tender's Hospital Visit

David sat down in the kitchen, and I played him the message.

"Good afternoon, David and Elaine, this is Loriann. Tomorrow is Saturday, and Anne and some of her friends are going to the arcade and bowling alley. Elaine, would you and Tender want to join us for some fun?"

Tender heard the sound of the machine from down the hallway and came running. "Oh, please, could we, Mom?" she begged.

"Tender, I thought you were asleep. Yes, I will call Loriann and find out what time they are leaving," I said, shooing her down the hall.

I called Loriann and found out the details. We agreed that we would join them.

In the morning, David watched us get ready and

moaned, "I wish I could go. Oh, if only the lawn could mow itself.." We all laughed.

"Tender, Loriann told me that the arcade opens at 10 AM, and we're going to meet them inside after we have our breakfast."

We all went for breakfast at the Eveready Diner. David ordered the family feast, which includes all-you-can-eat pancakes. Tender had two, I had three, but David had seven. By the time we finished eating, we had been there nearly an hour and a half, because David had to talk to everyone who dropped in at the diner. Tender and I enjoyed meeting David's friends; the only problem was that he always stood up and hugged everyone, and then talked to each person for several minutes. Tender and I would just say, "Nice to meet you." Finally, David went back home to do the yard chores, and Tender and I were off to the arcade. We arrived a few minutes after 10 AM. Anne ran up to Tender and hugged her. Tender knew most of the kids, as she had met them at Anne's parties. The moms were all there too, and we ladies were having fun, talking and watching our children at the same time. At lunchtime, we ordered pizza and drinks for everyone to enjoy.

After lunch, all the kids returned to the arcade. Tender and Anne especially loved the arcade bowling. I got up and was walking over to Tender to watch her, since I didn't often get to see her act like a kid. Suddenly, a big man, about six foot six inches and as big as a refrigerator grabbed Tender and threw her several feet in the air! She cried out, "Mom!" as she hit the floor hard.

My blood pressure must have went sky-high. I ran over to the man, as he threw a punch at me. I ducked and then spun into a roundhouse kick, planting my foot into the side of his face and knocking him to the ground. Then I yanked his arm behind his back and twisted his wrist upward so that he was unable to move. Meanwhile, Loriann ran over to Tender to see how she was doing. The police were called and informed that Tender was injured. They said they would send an ambulance, which arrived at the same time as the police. They showed up in force and arrested the man, a Frank Hanlon. His daughter was also taken to the police station. I called David, who had just got in from mowing the lawn, and told him that Tender had been assaulted and to meet us at the hospital. The mother of Frank's daughter came in to pick her up, and the police questioned her.

"Mrs. Hanlon, can you explain why your husband—"

"My ex-husband!" she exclaimed, irritably. Then

she turned to her daughter. "Donna, honey, why did Daddy hit that girl?" she asked, putting her hand on her daughter's shoulder.

"I wanted to play the bowling game, and she would not get off." Donna, howled and stomped her foot then crossed her arms over her chest.

"I am sorry, officer; as you can see, my daughter can be demanding, and my ex-husband spoils her," the mother said with a scowl.

The interrogating officer sighed and said, "Ma'am, you and your daughter may leave, but you should try to teach your daughter to be more patient."

"Yes, sir," she said meekly.

Meanwhile, when David reached the hospital, he was surprised that Tender was in a private room. His blood boiled when he saw his daughter's injured hand and bruised face on the whole right side. Tender patted his hand and told him it looked worse than it actually was. David said he would go see if the man would like to try picking on someone his own size.

"Dad, I don't want you to do that. Mom took care of the mean man," exclaimed Tender.

I came over and hugged David. With tears in my eyes, I told David how scared I had been for Tender.

Before we could say another word, over twenty

FBI agents showed up, including Agent Sisson and Director Lance. I gave them all a hug, with tears still in my eyes. When they saw Tender's injuries, they were all furious. Big John came into Tender's room, and he started crying, putting his hands over his face. After he composed himself, he went and sat on the edge of her bed.

"Tender, sweetie, are you, okay? Just let me get my hands on that guy, and he will never lay hands on a child again!" Big John growled, thumping his fist into the palm of his other hand.

"You sound like my dad," Tender replied with a weak smile.

Meanwhile, with all the attention on Tender, Director Lance asked to speak to David and me in private. We agreed, so we went down to the hospital cafeteria.

"Director, how did you know about Tender being attacked?" asked David.

"At headquarters, we have several agents manning the local police scanners throughout the state. When we heard that one of our own was injured, we sent a team over. I immediately contacted the hospital and informed them that an agent was on their way in; that's why they were waiting outside for Tender to arrive," he explained, putting a reassuring hand on my shoulder.

"I thought she resigned from the FBI," David asked, putting his hands on his hips.

"Listen, what I am about to tell you must stay confidential. Tender is an official FBI agent. When she was awarded an FBI badge, she received full power, and it was signed by the Secretary of Defense. Tender receives a full paycheck every month, put in a trust fund for her until she is twenty-one years old. I do not have the power to accept her resignation. In order for her to resign, she would need to send a letter to the Secretary of Defense, explaining why she wants to leave. However, I want to apologize for my behavior that day; I was having a family problem. I want to inform you that next week we are raiding that compound in Texas, sending in our best agents. Are we okay?"

I smiled at Director Lance and gave him a big hug.

"There is one thing Tender would like as a condition for her return," David said, his hands still on his hips.

"Anything," Director Lance answered earnestly.

"Starting next week, we would like to have Agent John Riley assigned to Team Purdy. Also, we want the option to pay him extra when he helps us solve a case. This will get Tender back to helping the FBI solve very difficult cases as well as give her better protection," David requested.

"I will speak to the top brass about it on Monday. One more thing: Frank Hanlon is now in FBI custody for assaulting an agent. We will investigate every possibility to see if he is wanted anywhere else in the country," said Director Lance in an angry voice.

David finally smiled at Director Lance and shook his hand. As we headed upstairs, we could hear laughter coming from Tender's room.

Tender's doctor came bustling in. "This is the most popular room in the hospital!" she exclaimed. "Has anyone seen my patient?"

The doctor moved over to Tender's bed. "Tender, is it true you are an FBI agent?" she asked.

Before she could answer, several agents yelled, "Yes, she is, and she is the best agent in the country." All the agents clapped in agreement.

The doctor then turned to us and continued, "Mr. and Mrs. Purdy, the good news is that the X-ray showed no broken bones. The bruise on her face is minor and will heal soon. You may take her home as soon as we sign her out."

Director Lance whispered in David's ear, and then he briefly left the room, returning in about five minutes.

David said, "Okay, honey, let's get you home."

Tender thanked all the agents for coming to

make sure she was okay. "I am tired and just want to rest," she said as she smiled around the room.

"Thank you, everyone, for going beyond the call of duty for Tender," I said, as tears came into my eyes again.

All the agents and some of the police officers stood in two lines and saluted Tender as she was wheeled out. When Tender went by Big John, she shouted, "See you tomorrow at 9 AM at the Eveready Diner."

"Yes, you will," Big John yelled back. As Tender was passing Director Lance, he leaned down and handed Tender back her badge. She looked up at me, and I signed "ok" in sign language.

Finally, we were on our way home, with police cars and FBI vans escorting us home, sirens blazing, right to our front door. Every single neighbor stopped by to inquire what all the commotion was about. When I explained what had happened, they were shocked and then wished Tender a fast recovery. Calls started coming in from family and church friends. Pastor Bob and his wife, Jackie, came by to pray over Tender.

David drove over to headquarters to meet with Frank Hanlon. He was allowed into Frank's holding cell with an FBI agent escorting him.

"My name is David Purdy, and it was my daughter you injured," David said with a stern frown.

"I am so sorry. I acted like a fool." Frank said, covering his face with his hands.

"I wish I had been there, because it would have been you that was taken away in an ambulance," David growled.

"I am so, so sorry. Please tell your daughter I regret my actions, and I hope she is okay," Frank moaned.

"I appreciate your apology, but I am still angry that my little girl had this awful experience," David said. Then he turned and left, still fuming.

A Strange Man at the Door

When David pulled up at home, there was a strange-looking man sitting on our doorstep. He was very short, no more than five feet six inches tall. He had a scar on his right cheek and a scar over his left eye, and his nose was out of place, like it had been broken. But the most distinctive feature was that he was missing a piece of his left ear. He looked familiar, but David just couldn't place this battered man. He looked confused and had trouble speaking. His eyes were so red that David's first thought was that he was on drugs, so David approached cautiously. "May I help you, sir?" David asked, as he stood sideways in a defensive stance.

"Mr. Purdy," he began, and then he stopped and put his hands over his face. "You don't know me. My name is Andrew Masson, and my wife is Allie.

I am from Dover, Delaware. Three years ago, my baby girl was kidnapped from her grandparents' house, Norman, and Helen Masson. I need your help. Please let me tell you what happened.

He invited him in. Tender was resting quietly on the couch. I introduced myself to Andrew Masson, and he explained with tears in his eyes that his daughter was still missing.

I went and got him some tissues and a glass of water.

Tender remained quiet on the couch.

"Please tell us everything that you can remember," said David, offering the man a seat.

"On Saturday, May 5, 1962, Allie and I were celebrating our five-year anniversary. We decided that every five years we would take a vacation. This being our first trip, we decided to spend seven days in Hawaii. We had left on Thursday, May 3, and left our two-year-old deaf daughter Meagan with my deaf parents, Norman and Helen Masson. My parents own a ranch house, so it would have been easy for someone to enter the house, since my parents would not hear any noise."

Tender sat up and asked, "So how did they get in?"

"Whoever it was, they somehow came in without breaking in. They didn't even leave any fingerprints.

When my parents woke up the next morning, Meagan was gone." Andrew started to cry. "Please help us; this is tearing us apart. My little girl would be five years old now."

I handed him some more tissues as he wept quietly.

David asked, "How did you know to contact us?"

"I have an uncle who works on the Bismarck police force. His name is Ben Masson, and he said your little girl is special," Andrew replied, blowing his nose.

"That she is. We have not worked with your uncle, but he is a sergeant in the S.W.A.T. division, and a great person," David said enthusiastically.

"Please say you will help. I have no way to pay you, as I have spent all my money on private detectives," Andrew said with a moan.

Tender said, "We will take your case. Please meet us on Monday at FBI headquarters, at 10 AM"

Andrew looked up gratefully. Then he noticed Tender's injuries. "What happened to you?" he gasped.

"A mean man hurt me, but my mom got him good!" Tender explained shortly.

"I am sorry that happened to you" Andrew said sympathetically.

"Do you have a place to stay for the night?" I

asked. We did not have a lot of room to spare, but I couldn't turn him out on the street.

"Yes, I am staying with my Uncle Ben," Andrew nodded at me.

"Oh, I'm so glad to hear it. And he can help you get to headquarters," I said, relieved.

"Mr. Masson, you told me you have a copy of the file on your daughter's disappearance with you?" David asked.

"Yes, it's in my car," Andrew said. He went out to his car and brought it back. "I will leave it with you to look over. But for now, I should be getting back to my Uncle Ben's place."

We bid him good night, promising him we would see him on Monday morning.

Once he was gone, I said to David, "I have never seen a face as scarred as Mr. Masson's."

Tender closed her eyes, using her recall. "Andrew Masson, three-time lightweight boxing champion of the world. His last title was in April 1962; the following month, his daughter was taken."

David jumped up and pumped his fist into the air. "I was sure that I knew him from somewhere."

"Daddy, promise me you will never go into boxing." Tender pleaded, eyeing David warily.

"Never! My face is way too pretty to be a punching bag," he grinned. He struck a pose like he was a model.

"So, David, you think your face is pretty?" I teased, smiling at him. "Tender, what do you think?"

"I don't know, Mom; maybe with some rouge and some bright red lipstick, Daddy could be a pretty man on the police force." Then she and I both burst out laughing. David didn't say a word, he just continued to pose.

After we had calmed down, David said, "Okay, enough joking around. Let's get back to Mr. Masson."

After reviewing the file for just a few hours, Tender was ready to present it to the FBI. Then we all went to get a good night's sleep.

Tender and I got up first, as David headed to the shower. After getting ready, we headed out to pick up Mrs. Hines and Skippy to go to the Eveready Diner. When we got there, Big John was already there waiting for us.

"Good morning, Big John," we all said happily.

"Tender, you look a little better this morning," Big John smiled.

"I feel much better, thank you." Tender smiled back.

Everyone at the diner had heard about Tender's encounter yesterday, and the staff at the diner were all angry. I think if they could have gone to confront Frank Hanlon, whom they knew very well, they would have given him a piece of their mind.

During the sermon at church, Pastor Bob used Tender's injuries as an example of the Good Samaritan. He spent the next forty-five minutes summarizing why we should be a good neighbor to others. Then he asked, "Who was a good neighbor to Tender? Was it not her FBI and police friends, her dad, and especially the mother lion who takes care of her baby cub?"

After the church service, Big John went up to meet Pastor Bob. Big John confessed to Pastor Bob that he stopped coming to church because he was mad at God after his beloved wife passed away. Pastor Bob was kind and gentle with Big John and promised to pray for him daily. All Big John said was that he would be back.

Today the family gathering was at our house. David and the men clustered around the grill, each demanding that it was their turn to cook the hot dogs and burgers this week. Just as Tender predicted, Grandpa Jake came over and grabbed the spatula right out of David's hand, announcing, "Okay, all you amateurs, let the master show you how it is done."

Grandpa's grilling was always amazing. He would gather the kids around him and say, "To get the perfect hamburger, cook it for five minutes on one side, and another five minutes on the other side, only flipping it once. But don't tell your dads." Then the kids would all laugh and run off to play.

Big John enjoyed our family games. We always played men against women., the men would not let Tender play trivia games. But if she ran by, she would give us ladies an answer to a tough question or two.

After most people had gone home, David called a team meeting. Mary and Richard were there too. "Big John, would you join us please?" called David.

"Yes, I sure can," he said as he followed us into the living room.

"John Riley, we held a meeting the other day. If you are interested, we would like you to join our team," announced David.

"Well, now, what would that entail me doing, and would it be a paying job?" Big John asked, shrewdly.

"We would ask you to help with research, stake-outs, or whatever else is needed to solve a case. You will receive 10 percent of any of our rewards," David answered.

"Will this be a full-time position?" Big John inquired.

"Yes. You can think it over, Big John. Next week, you can let the team know what your answer is," David said.

"No need to wait. I have been thinking of asking

you to consider putting me on your team. Although I have to say, I will regret retiring from the FBI." Big John smiled as Tender grabbed his hand.

"Well, don't retire yet. We have been working on a plan for you to be assigned to work as an FBI liaison with the Bismarck police force and Team Purdy," David smiled.

"No way," Big John boomed out. Then he laughed happily.

"Okay, team. Let's all do our jobs on Monday, and then meet back here at 4 PM," David said.

"Big John, are you still suspended without pay?" I asked.

"Yes, I am. But it's no problem; I can afford a few weeks off without pay," Big John assured us.

"No, you will receive the same salary as you get at the FBI while on Team Purdy while you are not being paid by the FBI," David announced.

"All right, thank you, friends." Big John accepted gratefully.

We all hugged and said good night. Mary and Richard were as excited as we were to have Big John on board.

On Monday, after breakfast, David, Tender, and I reported to the police station first. We informed Chief Purdy about the new case with Andrew Masson. He needed to know when we were working with the FBI, so they could bill the hours.

We arrived at headquarters a little early, but Mr. Masson was already there, waiting for us. Tender walked up to the front desk and attempted to show her FBI identification to the new front desk staff, but the woman was distracted and did not see it. She missed saying hi to Big John.

"Would you be as so kind as to sign in, and I will have an agent escort you to your destination," the lady at the front desk demanded. Tender put her FBI badge back in her pocket and started to walk toward the elevator. The lady yelled after her, "Young lady, I don't know what game you think you are playing here, but without signing in you may not enter the building."

Tender turned around quickly. "You are new here at headquarters. You recently finished your training. You were just married last month, and you moved here from Garland, Texas. Last night you slept on the floor. Dad, please give her some money, as she and her husband are flat broke until her first payday. You can pay us back next month, and if you need more, just ask. Linda, please tell your husband, Jim, that the Purdys said hi," she said, without missing a beat.

Linda just stood there with her mouth open in amazement.

Just then, Director Lance entered. "Good

morning, Purdys. Linda, I see you have met Agent Tender Purdy."

Linda never spoke a word. David left money on her desk as we passed by. David and I smiled at each other, knowing Tender had just done it to another person who underestimated her. David grabbed Tender's arm as she was walking. "Honey, how could you know so much about Agent Linda Carpenter? She gave you no hints."

"Dad, I asked Big John all about her, once I knew he was no longer manning the front desk," Tender smiled and winked mischievously. David and I started laughing.

Director Lance asked what was so funny. David explained what had just happened. He also joined in on the laughter as he patted Tender's head.

While we were in the elevator, Director Lance told us he was meeting with the top brass about you know who. We walked with him to his office, anxious to discuss our new case. However, he refused to talk about it and said he needed to speak to Tender alone first. So, David and I stepped outside the office. Meanwhile, Mr. Masson was patiently sitting in the waiting room, which had two agents posted at the door.

Inside the office, Director Lance was about to apologize when Tender interrupted him.

"Wait. I know why you were feeling stressed that day. Your beautiful wife of thirty years, Helen, was in the middle of major surgery. I noticed you were shaking and your palms were sweating. Now, that she is healing and is expected to have a full recovery, you are at peace with God," Tender reported, squeezing Director Lance's hand reassuringly.

Director Lance fell back in his chair with his mouth open. "How did you know all that?" he asked weakly.

"I could smell the operating room smell on your clothes that day. I suspect you followed her to the operating room and said goodbye at the operating room door. She only had a fifty-fifty chance of surviving open-heart surgery," Tender said compassionately.

Director Lance started to cry. "The thought of losing my wife was unbearable," he said. After a while. Tender went over and hugged him.

After a short while, Director Lance invited David and me back in.

"Okay, let's get to business," Director Lance said. "Please tell me about your new case now."

David explained the case, and Tender showed the director the evidence on Meagan. After reviewing the file, Director Lance was pleased to give his approval, and he signed off on the case. He called in Agent Sisson and ordered him to get his top team ready.

David went to the waiting room and informed Andrew Masson that we were on the case, asking him to follow me to the investigation room. Mr. Masson was unable to speak through his tears, his eyes red from crying. Once upstairs in the investigation room, Mr. Masson noticed all the agents always addressed Tender as Agent Tender Purdy.

Mr. Masson asked me in a whisper, "Is she is a real FBI agent?"

"Yes. She solves cases for the FBI and has all the same privileges of any agent, including bringing cases to the director," I answered with a smile. "Now that the director has given the okay, based on the evidence Tender presents today, you could have FBI agents working on your case by the end of today," I explained, patting his arm.

"But the FBI already failed to find my little girl." said Mr. Masson angrily. "How will this be any different?" I kept silent and waited for Tender to begin.

Tender went and stood at the podium made specially made for her. "Good morning, agents. We have a kidnapping case to investigate. Meagan Masson, the five-year-old daughter of this gentleman here, Mr. Masson, was removed from her grandparents' home in the middle of the night three years ago when she was only two years old. I have all the answers on what happened. After reviewing the crime scene photos, I have determined how she was removed from the house while all the windows and doors were still locked." Mr. Masson was leaning forward to listen intently.

"One of the photos of the back of the house shows a metal bulkhead. The kidnappers used a powerful magnet to open this bulkhead. We have this same type of bulkhead at our house, so my dad and I used a powerful magnet on it, and we were able to open the bulkhead. Then we noticed the paint on our bulkhead was all scratched afterward. The bulkhead at the house of Mr. Masson's parents has these same scratches. We also determined this process was very noisy, and anyone in the home would have heard it—unless the family was deaf. You see, Mr. and Mrs. Masson were in Hawaii for their fifth wedding anniversary. Mr. Masson's totally deaf parents were watching Meagan. So, they would not have heard anyone getting in through the bulkhead by unlocking it, removing the child, and leaving through the same bulkhead and locking it back up with a magnet. Since the kidnappers were wearing gloves, they left no fingerprints behind."

"So, what clues do we have?" asked Agent Sisson

"The child was removed on Thursday, May 3, sometime in the evening. This means the child was abducted while the Massons were in flight. How did the perpetrators know the flight schedule? They also had to know the grandparents were deaf. That's a lot of information for someone to have," Tender listed.

Tender continued.. "I want to get a list from every post office that filed a change of address from May 1 to May 15 of that year. We should note anyone who filed one in this time period; it might be them that has the Masson's girl. After you have the list, Mr. Masson will review the list to see if he identifies anyone on it."

Tender looked at Director Lance. "Tender are you convinced this case is worthy of a second look?" he asked her.

"Yes please."

"Ok, we are going to get this family back together," Director Lance promised.

"One more thing. When you enter the house of the kidnappers, please remember that the little girl is deaf, so please have someone on hand that knows sign language."

"Thanks for the tip. We will be sure to do that," Director Lance assured her.

"Once she has been returned here, I can sign

with her," Tender replied. Mr. Masson hugged Tender with tears in his eyes. "Thank you so much," he replied with a choked-up voice.

"Don't thank me yet, not until we have your daughter home safely." Tender replied, hugging him back.

Then Mr. Masson filled out the needed FBI forms and gave me his contact information so we could be in touch.

Two weeks later, the FBI contacted David and me to report that they had found the missing girl in the state of Washington. From there we flew her to Bismarck for processing. "The kidnappers were people Mr. Masson had met in the hospital one day; he remembered that their baby had died at birth. He had gotten their address and mailed them a sympathy card. He and his wife developed a friendship with them. After a few years, they noticed the other couple was starting to get too attached to their little girl. They decided to end the friendship about six months before the kidnapping happened. They never suspected that these former friends would plot against their daughter." Director Lance reported.

The FBI asked us to fly to Delaware, on their private jet, with Director Lance and Agent Sisson, along with Meagan, who was now six years old, to return her to her parents' home. On the plane, Tender and her new friend Meagan used sign language to communicate.

"Mom, she is very smart, and she remembers her mother and father. She was told that they had died in a plane crash while on their trip. They also told her that they had been assigned guardianship if anything happened to her parents, since they were best friends," Tender explained.

Agent Sisson asked, "Tender, how did you learn sign language?"

"The Montessori school where I attend requires every student to learn to sign. Just like at my mother's school, if any of the students are deaf, the teachers would teach all the students in sign language. And even when they were not in their classroom, every student was required to use sign language. This practice leaves no student out of the conversation," Tender replied.

"That's wonderful." Agent Sisson replied, smiling at Tender.

Once the plane landed, we headed over to the FBI headquarters in Dover. I was excited for Meagan. Tender held her hand since she was very nervous. As soon as she saw her family, everyone started to cry. Her mother fainted, but the FBI had medical team on hand just in case they were needed.

When her mom came to, they hugged one another and clung to their daughter like they would never let her go. I looked at Tender and realized she was crying too, so I went over and gave her a big hug.

After a while everyone began to calm down and we said goodbye. We exchanged addresses because Meagan wanted to be Tender's new pen pal. The Massons felt awful as they were unable to present us with any reward for finding Meagan but were happy to hear there was a standard FBI reward for recovered missing persons. We stayed the day in Dover, and the next morning, the FBI flew us home. Tender looked very comfortable, leaning back in the airplane seat, as she said, "Hey, Dad, we need to get one of these jets."

Everyone laughed, and Director Lance said, "If you keep this up, you will someday."

Finally, we arrived home. Tender was exhausted from all the excitement and was glad the next day was Saturday.

We had missed our Monday night meeting, so we rescheduled it for the next day. Late Saturday afternoon, Mary, Richard, and Big John all came over. The reward money was given out and everyone was pleased. After chatting and catching up about the Masson case, we all headed to the investigation room.

Mary, Richard, and Big John had new information to report on the cold case of the hit-and-run.

"David, you will be proud of us. We have the name and address of the suspect, and we have had the Corvette impounded. We explained to the owner that we will tell him why we had to take the car after we are done with our investigation," explained Big John, twirling his pencil in his fingers.

"The examination of the car revealed that the original paint color was Matador Red. The kicker was that with close examination, they found small patches of the paint from the Chevy Nomad, when they carefully removed some of the new paint." Richard continued, leaning back in his chair.

"The owner was the only person who refused to answer any questions when we called him. His name is Eric Mahoney, and he lives in Fargo," Mary finished.

Big John informed us that the raid of the compound in Texas was postponed until next week, as Director Lance wanted Tender to direct the raid.

"Any word on my being relocated to Team Purdy?" asked Big John anxiously. He kept twirling his pencil, and I realized he was more anxious about it than he let on.

"No, not yet." I responded. "Director Lance is still waiting to hear back from the top brass."

David pulled checks out of his wallet. He paid Mary and Richard their hourly wage, and he paid Big John his share of the reward from the last case, and his hourly wage.

Everyone was chatting happily when Tender said, "Please pray for Vicky Smith, that she will be brought home safe." We all became quiet, and then David led us all in a group prayer for Vicky's safe return.

By now it was getting late, so Big John left to go home, and David took Mary and Richard home. "See you all in the morning at the Eveready Dinner at 9 AM," Tender called after them as they left.

Sunday was Tender's favorite day of the week. We picked up Mrs. Hines and Skippy before breakfast. When we arrived at the Eveready Diner, Big John was outside waiting for us as he wanted to help Mrs. Hines inside. Big John was always extra kind to kids and seniors. He wasn't as friendly with adults who gave him a difficult time.

Once inside the diner, our family ordered breakfast. This week, Big John insisted on being treated as part of the family and paid for the meal. Every week, anyone can offer to pay the bill, but the rule is that you can't volunteer to pay again until next month.

After church, we all headed to Grandpa and

Grandma's house. Grandma made her famous pot roast. After lunch, Big John went outside to watch the kids play with Skippy. Once Skippy saw Tender, he never left her side. The men were watching a basketball game on television. Us ladies were finishing cleaning up the kitchen and giggling loudly. After the basketball game ended, Grandma yelled, "Now it's time for dessert, and then it's game time."

When the trivia game started, Big John insisted that Tender be allowed to play this time. All the men started to complain and grumble, but when Big John stood up, they suddenly stopped their complaining. "Only if Tender can answer every other question," they begged. The women were fine with that. Tender had only one weakness: she wasn't as good at answering sports questions. The men finally won a few games, but the women won more.

As the day wound down everyone grabbed a little more food and said their goodbyes . Mrs. Hines was getting tired, and even Skippy was sleeping in Tender's lap. I invited Big John, Mary, and Richard over for popcorn and a movie. David offered to have Mary ride home with us, but she wanted to ride with Richard, as he had just bought his own car with some of the money they had earned. It was a 1961 Chevy Impala, with an 8CYL 283 170HP

4-barrel carburetor. It was a white convertible with a blue stripe and a blue-and-white interior. It had cost him $800.

When we dropped Mrs. Hines off safely at her home, Big John would always go around to check the house, even the basement. While he was checking around Tender noticed that Mrs. Hines was favoring her left side when she walked. So, Tender and I went inside to check her left leg. Mrs. Hines laid down on the couch.

"Grandma Hines, where does your leg hurt?" asked Tender anxiously.

Mrs. Hines pointed to the back of her leg. Tender felt her left calf muscle.

"Does this hurt, Grandma?"

"Yes." she replied in pain.

"Tender is she going to be all right?" asked Big John, who had just come up from the basement. He also looked concerned.

"Yes, but there is some swelling, and it is tender to the touch. There is also some discoloration and redness, and it is warmer than usual," Tender explained.

"Should we bring her to the hospital?" I asked, now worried.

"No, Mom, but she will need to wrap her leg. She will need to ice her leg and then add heat three times a day. I also want her to take aspirin to thin her blood. This type of problem can cause blood clots," Tender prescribed.

"Sounds good. I will write up a schedule, and we will take turns coming over to help care for Mrs. Hines," I said briskly.

"Please call me Grandma, like Tender does," Mrs. Hines smiled up at me.

"Tender, how long should I ice and then heat it? I will do the night shift every time I can," said Big John, patting Mrs. Hines's shoulder.

I wrote down the instructions as Tender dictated them to me. Then I left the note on the coffee table.

"Grandma, we will have a family member come by in the morning to care for you during the day. Do you have any aspirin?" I asked.

"Yes, in the small medicine cabinet in the bathroom," she answered. I went and got it out for her and gave her one tablet, like Tender instructed. We said good night, and I also gave her one of our business cards with our phone number on it and reminded her to call us any time.

"No," boomed Big John. That will not do. I would like to bring over a change of clothes and sleep in the spare bedroom. What if she were to fall and not be able to get up? I can't let that happen on my watch" boomed Big John.

Tender went over and gave Big John a big hug,

"That is why you are my favorite. I love you, Big John," said Tender, squeezing him tight.

Tender had us head over to the hospital even though Dr. Turk wasn't on duty. We spoke to Dr. Turk over the phone, and he approved of wrapping her leg and also provided a hot water bag. Dr. Turk also wanted us to bring Grandma Hines to get checked out tomorrow at 4 PM. We returned to Grandma's house with the supplies just as Big John returned with his overnight bag, then we headed home

As soon as we got home, Tender headed to bed. She was exhausted but happy that Grandma was so well cared for.

David and I sat down in the living room with a cup of tea. I put my head on David's shoulder and started to cry.

"Are you okay, honey? What do you need?" David asked anxiously.

"I need to know why God chose us to be the parents of such a caring and loving little girl." I sniffled.

David took me in his arms. Holding my shoulders, he looked into my eyes. "Elaine, I need to know why you chose me to be your husband," he said, as tears started in his eyes.

"David, I dreamed from my childhood that I would have a family someday. I never thought I would have such a loving husband, beautiful daughter, and a family that makes me feel like I was born into the family. David, I love my life because you chose me."

David comforted me for a while, and before we knew it, we had both fallen asleep on the couch.

Early the next morning, we woke up to hear Tender yelling, "Mom, Dad, where are you?"

We both raced down the hall as fast as we could. Tender was standing outside our room, crying. "Where were you? I was afraid something happened to you." Tender sobbed.

I grabbed her and gave her a hug. "Tender, we fell asleep on the living room couch while we were winding down last night," I said.

"Well, don't do that again. I was afraid," Tender said. I looked at David, and we both smiled. As Tender and I went into the kitchen to get breakfast ready, David went to shower before work. David soon entered the kitchen eager for breakfast.

Tender wanted to stay with us today. "David," I whispered, "we need to remember she is still our little girl." David nodded his head yes because his mouth was full of food. So, we all headed over to police headquarters and had a meeting with Chief Purdy.

Chief Purdy was glad to see us. "Do you have any information about who owned the 1958 Matador Red Corvette?" he asked.

"Yes, but does the Attorney General believe we have enough evidence to get a warrant for an arrest based on the evidence found on the Corvette?" asked David.

"Absolutely—as soon as we have a name and address, we can issue a warrant for an arrest," nodded Chief Purdy.

"The suspect is Eric Mahoney, now living in Fargo, North Dakota," I was glad to report.

The Fargo police were notified about the warrant for Eric Mahoney. The police chief was surprised, because he knew Mr. Mahoney, who was an outstanding member of the community. However, he did wish us luck.

Chief Purdy informed us we were to report to FBI headquarters, so we drove over there. Once there, Tender just smiled at Linda Carpenter and waved.

"Tender, I have something for you." Linda beckoned. Then she whispered, "Please forgive me," as she handed Tender a rainbow pop. Just then, David put his hand out for a pop too, and she playfully slapped it. "Agents only!" Linda barked. Tender laughed. She was starting to like Agent

Carpenter. She had a strong build, and was very muscular for a woman.

In the elevator, I noticed David was still rubbing his hand from that slap. Tender and I smiled at each other, trying not to laugh. "He will never learn," I said to Tender.

Once we were upstairs, Director Lance and Agent Sisson were ready to explain how they wanted to approach the deaf commune.

"Okay, Purdys, here is the situation: we have a small town of one hundred residents located in Bill Hogg County, Texas. The sheriff and his deputy are going to assist us in the background. We pull out tomorrow; our plane leaves at 10 AM. We have over one hundred agents stationed in different towns located in Bill Hogg County. Team Purdy, how do we proceed?" asked Director Lance.

"For this case, we need to proceed with caution. I have read many books on various kinds of communes. However, since this is an all-deaf commune, we do not know what we are dealing with. Have you done surveillance on the grounds surrounding the property, and did you find the escape tunnel locations?" Tender asked.

"Yes, we used sound waves from low-flying planes. Here is a copy of the map," Agent Sisson said as he brought up a slide with a map of the commune.

Tender and I looked over the map for the longest time. "Wait a minute—I believe this is a trap. These tunnels might be rigged. They want us to enter through these tunnels, and if I am right they will blow them up, burying every agent alive inside," I exclaimed. Tender agreed.

"How do you know it is a trap?" asked Director Lance, his eyebrows raised.

"Mom, you go ahead," Tender nodded at me.

"You can see it on the arial map," I answered.

"What do you see?" the director asked.

Everyone looked closely, but they still didn't notice anything out of the ordinary.

"See the small circles on the surface of the tunnels?" Tender eventually pointed out.

"They look just like a pencil dot.,"

"Right. Those might be M14 land mines, still being used in the Vietnam War. If I were them I would place mines in various locations above the tunnels, just under the ground. Once all the agents are in the mines, they will shoot the mines from the flat roof of the building we are calling 'G,' Tender warned.

"We will have to find another way in," Director Lance said with a frown.

SEVEN

Tender and the Cult

Going home for the night was out of the question since we were on an active case. We had spare clothes in the lockers at headquarters. Tender was tired, so she went to bed in her FBI bedroom, with an agent standing guard all night. Tender said she wanted to ponder the escape plan, so she could find a way not to have innocent children injured, especially Vicky Smith.

Morning came quickly. We had breakfast in the FBI cafeteria, and then headed to the investigation room. The lead agents who would command this raid were ready for their orders, and the case was called 'Mother Goose.'

Tender and the ten special agents who would be leading the mission had paper and pencil in hand. As Tender had requested the night before, they were each given a small map with red dots showing the location of the mines.

"Everyone, listen up carefully, please. Notice the red dots on your map. These are land mines we believe are a trap to trick us, by going into the tunnels below these mines. The property and several buildings are located at an elevation of 640 feet, but the hillside is 680 feet, almost 40 feet higher. You will place a several agents, who are marksmen, along the perimeter and have them ready to start shooting at 1220 hours. Your high-ground agents, will start shooting the mines at the same time. Have them keep shooting until all the mines are set off," Tender instructed.

"When the mines start going off, just as the residents are about to have lunch, they will be unprepared, but it won't be long before they put their own plan into action. We will have the five helicopters drop off those agents onto the highest roof to protect the agents on the ground. They will need to be aware of the cult leaders trying to access that roof from a stairway. The helicopters should be equipped with bulletproof armor, which are easy to onload," Tender continued. Then she pointed to the leaders, "Don't mess this up!" She slapped her hands down on the table.

"Finally, and most importantly, I believe that

inside the largest building are military trucks ready to carry the residents off campus to a secret location set up to hide them away for years without coming out," Tender went on.

"Another important part will be knowing the path they will be forced to take. Most of the men will stay back to fight against us. Miles down the road, you will set up a roadblock. The caravan will be staffed by women only; they may have guns, and may be willing to die to evade capture. Please put your best agents at this location so no children are injured. May God be with you. You know I love you all," Tender said. I had never seen her look more serious.

We entered a military plane; the flight was a little rough, so I held Tender for the whole ride. She fell asleep and woke up a few hours before we landed. The agents took their jobs seriously, as all they did during the flight was study Tender's plan. We landed without a hitch. All the commanders had Jeeps ready to take the agents to their hotels in the area, housing ten men in each hotel. Agent Sisson had all the leaders ready from their positions. He visited every hotel post and went over that group's specific task.

The next morning, David, Tender, and I stayed back and prayed until we received a message from Agent Sisson:

'Mother Goose,' all your goslings are in the nest, safe and sound.

We all jumped for joy and hugged one another. Before long, we were escorted to the debrief location on a military base a few hours away. Once there, Tender and I went looking for Vicky Smith.

When Vicky saw me, she ran toward me, crying hysterically. She was so distraught that she had to be sedated, and was brought to the infirmary, along with 110 other hostages from the age of 6 months to 22 years old, with most being deaf.

EIGHT

What to Do with Vicky Smith?

Morning approached, and due to the noise on a military base, there was no sleeping-in after sunrise. We all headed down to the mess hall for the worst breakfast in history. There we met up with the brave FBI agents, who all stood up when Tender entered the hall. They started cheering, clapping, and chanting, "Tender! Tender! Tender!" for the longest time.

Tender stood on top of a chair and spoke to the men and women.

"I am so proud of every one of you. I was saddened to hear that over twenty of the people in the commune lost their lives. However, in *Matthew 26:52 Jesus says 'For all they that take the sword shall perish with the sword.' Jesus also says in John 15:13 'Greater love hath no man than this, that a man lay down his life for his friends'.*

All of the agents yelled, "Amen!"

Tender said, "For those who do not know the meaning of the word *Amen*, it means you are saying to God, 'I agree.' "

Tender wanted to visit Vicky as soon as she finished eating at the mess hall. "Now I understand why they call it a *mess* hall—because of the taste," she said, making a face. "Mom, how can Dad eat this food so fast?" Tender cringed.

"Darling, I think he is a robot and not human," I teased. David looked up, surprised that we were finished. "Really, David, you want more?" I said disbelievingly.

"It's not so bad, and I didn't eat at all yesterday!" David said around mouthfuls.

Tender and I both pushed our plates toward him. Tender observed that all the men ate everything on their plates, while the ladies picked at their food without interest. They would rather go hungry than eat that food.

After the meal, we were finally allowed to enter the infirmary and see Vicky. She was resting in an infirmary bed. She signed to Tender and me that if we had not come soon, she didn't know what would have happened. She thought the leaders of the commune believed, if Jacob from the Bible could go to Egypt with only seventy people and leave Egypt four hundred years later with over a million, then he wanted to do the same.

"Are you okay?" Tender signed back.

"Yes, now that you are here," Vicky signed as she let out a deep breath.

"Vicky, my name is Tender, and you knew my mom, as Elaine Smith now Purdy ." Vicky grabbed my hand and squeezed it tight.

"I remember you, Elaine, and I know who you are, Tender. I also know that if it wasn't for you, I would never have been freed. But I am surprised and confused that a girl like you could have anything to do with saving all of us?" Vicky shook her head in confusion.

"Vicky, I know it's hard to believe what Tender is capable of understanding, but trust me—there isn't one detail of the plan to free every one of you for which Tender didn't have an input," I signed.

"Wait, are you saying that even the FBI needs her help?" Vicky looked intently at Tender.

"Vicky, dear, not only is Tender an FBI agent, but she is also a lawyer and an unofficial doctor. Most of all, she loves helping those who are in trouble. The criminals who sold you to this cult also did this to fifty-nine other girls, but you were the only one the authorities could not find. They didn't have enough information on you to keep the case open for one girl, so they closed the case and called it a success. Tender used her FBI influence to put together this team of agents to find you. All she talked about every day was finding you," I signed.

Vicky started to cry, and then so did Tender. I held them both.

Then Tender did something I would have never expected, and I'm still not sure David understands.

"Vicky, how would you like to be my sister?" Tender signed.

I took a step back in surprise. David, unsure of what had just happened, threw his arms in the air and looked from Tender to Vicky to me in confusion.

"I don't understand what you mean," Vicky signed.

"I think she is asking if you would like to become Vicky Purdy," I signed with a smile.

Vicky buried her hands in her face and could not get control of her emotions. After a little while, she nodded her head to say yes.

David looked at me in fear. Since he did not understand sign language, he had no idea what had just happened. I stopped signing, as David was very confused.

"David, please sit down. I have some good news and some bad news; which do you want first?" I said, raising my eyebrows at him.

119

"The bad news." David said in fear.

"The bad news is that you will have to learn sign language," I reported, pulling a long face.

"I don't understand," David said, shaking his head.

"The good news is that Vicky is going to become Vicky Purdy, Tender's sister." I spoke quickly, anxiously awaiting David's response.

David gaped at me for a whole minute. Then, finally, he said, "Okay, you girls know best."

Vicky read his lips and jumped at David to give him a big hug.

Tender was delighted that we were going back home on a private jet with her new sister, Vicky. Tender and Vicky and I signed all the way home. David wasn't happy because he was left out of our three-way conversation.

We arrived home a couple days later than all the FBI agents, who had returned right away to their assignments. As we arrived at the airport, we were unaware that Tender had made the national news. Every newspaper in North Dakota had reporters at the airport who wanted to interview Tender. The FBI agents on the plane contacted headquarters and the Bismarck police to help clear the runway so we could get home. I was concerned about Tender's new fame.

Once the FBI and the police arrived, with every available officer and agent on duty, they informed every news outlet that Tender was off limits. Any attempt to interfere with the life of a five-year-old would immediately be shut down.

Tender spotted Big John as she exited the plane, and ran up to him. "Big John, how is Mrs. Hines doing?" Tender asked anxiously.

"She is doing great. She does not even need the wrap anymore," Big John smiled.

Tender said goodbye to all her friends on the plane. We were then escorted into an FBI armored vehicle. They took us straight to headquarters. All the agents, Director Lance, Agent Sisson, and Chief Purdy were there to greet Tender. There was so much excitement in the room, it felt like seeing a rock star first come on stage.

Big John helped Tender onto a bench as Vicky stood beside her. Tender then put up her hand up to stop the cheering. "This is why we do what we love," said Tender, putting her hand on Vicky's shoulder. "Ladies and gentlemen, I would like to introduce my new sister, Vicky. Soon to be Vicky Purdy!"

The crowd went wild, yelling and screaming, with agents wiping tears from their eyes.

"I want to thank you all for your support in

ridding this world of some very bad people," Tender shouted, with her hands raised high to say goodbye.

Finally, we were able to go home. We needed to get Vicky settled in and get our lives back in order. There was so much to do. The next morning, everyone slept late, since we were going to take the day off. We went to breakfast at the Eveready Diner and then we all went shopping to get Vicky her new bedroom furniture. We allowed her to choose many of her own things.

The next day, David had a meeting at headquarters with Director Lance at 10 AM. Vicky and Tender were getting along very well, and Tender now had a fan club. It was fun to watch her answer difficult questions and sign autographs whenever we went out.

As David entered headquarters on Friday morning, he heard a loud voice command, "Mr. Purdy, to the front desk, please."

"Good morning, Agent Carter," said David, walking up to the front desk with a smile.

"Where do you think you are going?" Agent Carter responded.

"I have been summoned by Director Lance, so I was heading upstairs," David responded.

"Not without an escort. What's more, without Tender and her badge, the elevator won't operate," she explained.

"Okay, I understand," said David, signing in as a guest.

Then Agent Carter handed him a rainbow pop. "This is from Agent John Riley, for a job well done. Sixty girls saved. That is very impressive."

David held the pop high in the air as if he had won an Olympic gold medal. He wanted to start licking his pop right away, but then he decided he would wait until after his meeting. Within minutes, an agent came down to escort him to Director Lance's office.

"Good morning, Mr. Purdy; my name is Andrew Lions. How did things end up for Agent Purdy and the 'Mother Goose' operation?" he asked with a smile.

"All went as planned," David reported.

"My dream is to work on Agent Purdy's team one day," Agent Lions said with a sigh.

"Someday, you just may," David replied, smiling back at him. Once they reached the eleventh floor, Agent Lions knocked on Director Lance's door and cracked it open. "David Purdy to see you, sir," said Agent Lions.

"Let him enter. Good morning, David, would you like some coffee, or maybe breakfast?" Director Lance asked.

"Coffee, black, please," David replied. Director

Lance called down to the cafeteria and asked for two black coffees to be sent up.

"David, I just have a few things to discuss at this meeting. First, congratulations on the successful completion of the 'Mother Goose' operation. It is amazing the way Team Purdy solves the most difficult cases without many injuries." Then he smiled. "Also, your request for Agent John Riley as your liaison has been approved," Director Lance said.

"Yes! Thank you, sir," said David. He raised both his hands high into the air as if he had just scored a touchdown.

"We also have a surprise for Agent Riley. This Sunday at 1P.M., at the Bismarck Country Club, we will officially announce his promotion as Special Agent John Riley, liaison to investigating Team Purdy of the Bismarck Police Department. He will be working under Chief Purdy, and Chief Purdy will have to officially assign Special Agent John Riley to the unsolved cases team."

"That is fantastic news. What do you need us to do for Sunday?" asked David.

"I know that every fourth week, you and your family go out to different family home to eat. We have arranged for your whole family, including Mrs. Hines and Skippy to join us, so please make sure no one spills the beans about Sunday," Director Lance said.

"Finally, because Tender went above and beyond her duty in order to save 110 Americans from a life of hell, the Defense Department has issued a reward. Twenty-six of the families also contributed reward money. The total reward money is $10,000," Director Lance announced.

David nearly fell off his chair and hit the floor. Director Lance stood up and looked over at him.

"David Purdy, are you okay?" Director Lance asked.

"Yes," he wheezed as he took the checks. He wiped his forehead with his hand.

"David is Tender happy she found Vicky Smith?" asked Director Lance.

"Is she ever! She now has an older sister," David replied, still in shock about the reward money.

"That is wonderful news. My wife and I are considering adopting one of the younger children born at the commune. Did you know Elaine is contacting couples to see if they would consider adopting one of the many young children who were born at the compound and whose parents were killed in the raid?" Director Lance asked.

"No, but it doesn't surprise me. Just think—you

could end up with a Tender yourself," said David with a grin. They both laughed.

"That would be exciting, but I believe God made only one Tender," the director said.

They shook hands, and the director held on for a few extra seconds as he looked David in the eyes. "You Purdys are making a difference in this world. Thank you so much." They hugged, and then David left. He went back to police headquarters enjoying his rainbow pop. Once there he reported to Chief Purdy.

"Good morning, Chief Purdy. I apologize, but Elaine is going to need a few days off. We have decided to adopt Vicky and finally give her a home. Elaine, Tender, and Vicky are heading out to see Sister Mary Ellen in Lincoln to get the paperwork started for adopting Vicky. Then she will be meeting with our attorney to complete the adoption of Vicky and set a court date to finalize the adoption," David said.

"That's wonderful of you and Elaine to bring another child into your family. After all, the last one worked out great," Chief Purdy said warmly.

"I do have some bad news you are not going to like," David warned.

"You know I don't like bad news," the Chief responded gruffly, crossing his arms over his chest.

"Tender has decided the whole family should learn sign language every Sunday for the next year." David took a step back.

"Well, that won't be me. I will just ask someone to tell me what is being said," Chief Purdy said with a scowl.

"Tender's second rule is that no one is allowed to interpret what is being signed," David said, shaking his head.

"Well, we will see who holds more power in this family," retorted Chief Purdy. Then they both laughed.

"Chief Purdy how is the case of the 1958 Chevy going?" asked David.

"We had two warrants issued. First, we searched Eric Mahoney's property and found nothing out of the ordinary. Then we put a warrant out for his arrest. The FBI put out an APB with a top warrant poster on Eric Mahoney throughout the country. We haven't tracked him down yet, though. The sad thing is that after interviewing his co-workers, his family, and his friends, it sounds like he is a real nice guy who made a bad choice in 1962," the Chief said.

"These are the cases we all hate, because we will never know what would have happened if he had stayed and assisted in helping those victims," David replied sadly.

"On a good note, the town council has approved our new department budget," Chief Purdy reported proudly.

"Did the town council also approve having an FBI liaison installed as a member of the police force?" David asked nervously.

"Yes, since it was at no cost to the town. One of the council members looked into this kind of arrangement in other locations throughout the country. He discovered at least ten of the larger cities find it very useful to have an FBI agent assisting the police," Chief Purdy nodded.

"On Sunday, at the Bismarck Country Club, the town council will swear in Special Agent John Riley to the Bismarck police force. On Monday, can you bring Tender by to help discover where Eric Mahoney could be?" the Chief asked, consulting his calendar.

"Will do. How about first thing in the morning?" David asked.

"That works for me. And now, come and see your newly remodeled investigation room." Chief Purdy led the way down the hall.

David was in shock when he entered the room. It was the largest investigation room in the precinct, with a center chalkboard as well as a large cork board and hundreds of pins, in all different colors.

On the right was one large rolling notepaper board. At the front, there were two podiums, one for Tender with three steps, and one for an adult with no steps. But what made the room stand out even more was that it was painted Tender's favorite color, pink. David looked at the Chief and blurted out, "Pink!"

Chief Purdy laughed. "If it weren't for Tender, there would be no special unsolved cases division. And now, your team needs to decide on one detective who will be added to your division. I am going to post the position this afternoon. Your team will have to decide in the next couple months," the Chief smiled.

David asked to have the rest of the day off and Chief Purdy granted it willingly. David headed to the bank and deposited all the checks. Later in the afternoon, Tender, Vicky, and I returned with good news. Sister Mary Ellen was so happy to see Vicky, and to know all four of her missing girls would have wonderful homes. She awarded us temporary guardianship and filled out the forms for Vicky. Vicky was so excited to see her friends at the school again.

I had gone to the lawyers, and on Wednesday David and I would both need to go and sign the adoption papers, giving us full guardianship of the new Vicky Purdy. After that, we would have to wait a while before we could go to a family court judge to declare the adoption official.

David said he had announcements to make. "Okay, honey, I need you, Tender, and Vicky to sit down and be ready to be surprised." All three of us sat down on the couch, holding hands. Vicky would have to read David's lips until he learned to sign, or we interpreted.

When David saw we were ready, he continued, "There were twenty-seven different rewards for the safe return of those children."

"Okay, David how much?" I asked eagerly. David just smiled as he held up the deposit slip.

Tender yelled, "Is that $10,000?!"

I grabbed the slip. "That is crazy!" I gasped.

Vicky didn't understand and signed to Tender, "What is the money for?"

Tender signed back, "It is the reward money offered by parents, or sometimes by the FBI, for the safe return of their loved ones. We receive rewards all the time."

"Vicky, this money belongs to Team Purdy, of which you will now be a team member," I signed with a smile.

"I don't know what that means, but it sounds like fun," Vicky signed back.

"We need to have a team meeting. I have items

we need to vote on," said David. He began listing the items on the agenda. Meanwhile, Tender signed for Vicky, explaining what was going on.

"I do not know how to feel about this first request. Richard would like to use seven hundred dollars of their money to buy Mary an engagement ring. He intends to give it to her next month at their senior prom," David snorted.

"Did Grandpa Purdy give his blessing?" asked Tender.

"That's what bothers me—he gave in too easily," David replied, with his arms crossed in disgust. We all laughed because we girls were so happy for them.

"Well, I guess we don't have to vote. I am out-numbered!" David just wouldn't smile.

"No, we need to vote," I said, giving his arm a squeeze.

"Okay, then. Tender?" David called for votes.

"I vote yes," Tender said.

"Elaine?" I noticed David gave me a look as if he wanted me to say no.

"Yes! Yes! Yes!" I exclaimed, giving David a happy look.

"Vicky?" David asked, while Tender signed.

"Yes," she signed.

"Very well, the motion is approved." David just shook his head in disapproval.

131

Not long after our meeting, David ordered the pizza for the Friday night team meeting. Big John showed up first. He was so happy to meet Vicky. Richard and Mary arrived in Richard's new car. Richard was super excited to see the results of their efforts to find Vicky, but never in a million years did he think she would become a Purdy.

"Okay, David, tell me everything!" shouted Richard. Mary slapped Richard on the arm.

"Be patient, Richard. You know my brother will never give you so much as a hint. He does not believe in telling the same story twice," Mary laughed. Not long after they arrived, the pizza was delivered.

Mary was so excited to meet her new niece, even though they were only a few years apart. Vicky was just a few inches shorter than Mary. She was petite, with rather large arm muscles, blonde hair, blue eyes, and a baby face. She didn't look fifteen years old. Richard noticed that Vicky had very rough hands. He asked her, "What happened to your hands? Why are they so rough looking?"

"At the commune, I helped build a stone wall," Vicky signed back, and Tender interpreted for her.

"That explains the unusually large muscles for a girl your size," Richard said.

"We all worked hard," Vicky signed. After pizza, we headed to the living room for a team meeting.

"Let's get started. We have plenty of good news. First, the FBI, following Tender's instructions, was able to end the terror of this commune." said David briskly.

At this time, Vicky was asked to leave the room with Tender while David explained all the details of the mission. David did not want to scare Vicky with all the details. Big John, Richard, and Mary were shocked that if just one mistake had been made, the mission would have ended with many more injured or even dead. The girls were both invited back in after we discussed the case.

"Okay, now for case updates. Frank Hanlon, the man who attacked Tender, was wanted for other crimes, in several different states. For his arrest, we received another reward. Then there was also rewards from the 'Mother Goose' operation. Big John, here is your share of the money," David said, handing him an envelope.

"Holy moly!" Big John exclaimed. Then David handed Richard and Mary the same amount.

"Wow! I can't believe it Mary, soon we can buy a new house." Richard screamed.

"Richard Harris, don't you think we should be married before we buy a house?" Mary said, folding her arms over her chest just like her brother does.

"Why? We could buy one now, and I could fix

it up until we do get married," Richard said with a smile.

"What makes you so sure I will even say yes?" Mary fired off saucily.

"Oh, she will say yes," Tender interjected. We all laughed, except Mary and David.

"Finally, regarding our case of the hit-and-run with the 1958 Chevy Corvette and Eric Mahoney, Chief Purdy said they have searched his house, but nothing out of the ordinary turned up. All his family, friends, and work associates say he is a wonderful guy. There is an APB out on him as we speak," reported David.

"What is an APB?" asked Richard.

"Tender, do you want to answer this question?" said Big John with a smile.

"All Points Bulletin. That means if you go into any police station, post office, or FBI building, his picture will be on the bulletin board, and it will say WANTED on the top of the poster," Tender explained.

"I have seen those before at the post office," Mary said, nodding.

"Tender, on Monday morning, Chief Purdy would like you to come into the station to see if you can help locate Mr. Mahoney," David said.

"Okay, I can do that. And now, can we watch

a movie and have popcorn, Dad?" asked Tender with a grin.

"Yes, we can. Meeting adjourned." said David.

We all filed out of the living room and headed into the family room to watch a movie. Tender and Vicky liked sitting next to Big John, who would always nod off during our movie nights.

We all slept late on Saturday. I made breakfast, and then right after breakfast Tender got Vicky involved in a jigsaw puzzle. I explained that puzzles are a Purdy family favorite. Tender and her cousin Anne hold the record—in just under one hour they once finished a one thousand piece puzzle." I said.

"The only reason we finished it so quickly is because we had done the same puzzle several times." Tender signed.

"But don't worry," she assured Vicky, "it takes some family members months to finish one.."

"That's the men's average," I said, winking at Tender.

"Hey, I heard that." David yelled from the kitchen.

Then I explained to Tender and Vicky that we were going to get a present for Big John, and that there would be a surprise party for him tomorrow at the Bismarck Country Club. He would officially be on Team Purdy, starting Monday. "We are also picking up Richard, so I can go shopping with him," I said.

"Good. So, he is buying a diamond ring," Tender deduced.

On our way to go shopping, we picked up Grandma Purdy, as she also wanted to come along. She had to give Mary some chores to do so she wouldn't be able to come. After we picked up Grandma, we picked up Richard. He was fidgeting the whole time in the car, twisting his fingers, and tapping his feet.

"You look nervous," I commented. "Calm down, Richard. This will be fun."

David dropped off Grandma, me, and Richard at the jewelry store. We were laughing, but Richard still looked pale.

"Okay, girls, what do we get Big John?" asked David.

"We need to get him a trophy rifle," Tender answered immediately. Tender always knew what gift to give someone.

"All right let's head over to Big Game Hunting and Fishing," said David. He was glad he was going there instead of the jewelry store.

Since we only took the Mercedes and both David and I had a key, David, Tender, and Vicky decided to leave the Mercedes at the jewelry store and to walk to Big Game Hunting and Fishing. It took them about ten minutes to walk there. As soon as they were inside, a salesman approached David.

"Good afternoon, sir, my name is Luke Fleming. Are you shopping for yourself or for someone else?"

"Hi, Luke, my name is David Purdy, and these are my daughters, Tender and Vicky."

"Do you have any specials on rifles?" asked Tender.

"Are you Tender?"

"Yes sir."

"What a pretty name for a young lady. I don't believe you would know much about a rifle, now, would you?" Luke Fleming smiled.

"I bet my daughter knows more about any item in your store than the smartest salesman on the planet. How would you like to wager a free Redfield scope for our rifle?" said David, examining the store signs.

"Dad, please, I don't want you to lose any money over me," Tender replied.

The manager was walking by just then. He said, "I happened to overhear your conversation. If your daughter knows more than my salesman, you get your free Redfield scope. However, if my salesman knows more than her, you pay double for the scope. How old is she?" he said.

"She is only five years old, but you have a bet, sir," said David.

The manager went to the loudspeaker. "I have a knowledge challenge at post number one. Luke Fleming versus a five-year-old girl." He said as he chuckled. Many of the salesmen started to gather around. The manager brought back the specs on the Browning Automatic Military Rifle that we had asked to see, and the specs on the Redfield scope. He also brought back two notepads with pencils.

"Is it all right if I ask the questions?" David asked as he took hold of the specs.

"Fine with me," shrugged the manager.

Just then, Grandma, Richard, and I entered the store to see a large crowd surrounding Tender and a young man. I asked Vicky what was going on.

"Looks like they are going to lose a free scope," Vicky signed back. Then I explained it to Grandma, who only laughed.

"Here is my first question: What year was the first Browning Automatic produced?" David asked. Tender and Luke both answered, "1918." The manager and Luke, his son, were both surprised.

"Second question: How long is the barrel?" Luke wrote, "Twenty-four inches." Tender wrote, "609.6 millimeters or 24 inches long." They were both correct and the manager said, "She must be cheating." All the customers booed and yelled, "How can a five-year-old cheat?" He quieted down, knowing he was making his customers angry.

"Third question: Why did Browning make the Automatic, and what was it called?" Tender wrote, "The M196 was originally made for the military." Again, they both got it right. The crowd roared for Tender.

"Fourth question: What size caliber bullet does the rifle take?" Tender answered, "30.06." And again, they both got it right.

"Okay," the manager said, "since we are tied, you can each ask a question, and the person who answers wrong loses. Luke, you go first," said the manager, hoping to give him an advantage.

"Miss Tender, how many rounds a minute can the Browning Automatic fire?"

Tender answered, "The rifle can shoot 500 to 600, but it is rated at 550 rounds per minute." David held up the notebook.

"That is correct," said the manager. "Tender, you may ask your question."

"Luke, name the one outlaw who used the Browning Automatic rifle, committing crimes all over the country" Tender said.

Luke thought for a minute. "My guess is Al Capone," he said.

Tender shook her head and said, "It was Clyde Chestnut Barrow." Everybody started clapping. One of the store customers yelled, "How did you know all that, little girl?"

"My dad receives *American Rifle* magazine, and I have read every one of his magazines," Tender replied with a grin.

"That was amazing! You sure have one smart little girl there," the manager agreed.

"Well, follow me, and I will have you fill out the forms and get you on your way with a free Redfield scope," said Luke. Then he mumbled to himself, "I just know she cheats."

David paid for the rifle, and the store wrapped it up nicely with the scope.

"Tender, that was close. What would have happened if you lost?" I asked.

"Dad would have had to cough up double the cost of a Redfield scope. It is precision crafted, extraordinarily accurate, constantly centered, and easy to mount," Tender replied.

Just then, the manager turned around. "Young lady, you really do know a lot about firearms." he exclaimed.

"I told you I read a lot," Tender smiled at him.

"So, you're saying we never even had a chance?" he smiled back.

"Not even a little," said David, smiling too.

"Well, next time a child challenges us, I am going to decline," the manager snorted.

"Then you better take down that sign: 'If you know more about any item in our store than the smartest salesman on the planet, you get a free Redfield scope,' " I observed.

"Okay, then can I ask this little lady to make me a promise?" the manager asked.

"What is it?" Tender asked dubiously.

"Can you promise never to challenge any of my salesmen again? You were the first person to win a free item in a long time." he exclaimed.

"All right, that sounds fair. And I like you; you are funny." We all laughed.

After shopping, we all went to lunch. Later, in the afternoon, the whole team met for a jog. Big John is faster than he looks, but no one is faster than I am. One of the rules of Team Purdy is jogging for at least two miles a day to stay in shape. After our jog, we headed to the karate school. Lessons for the whole team are paid for by the newly formed Tender Purdy Company, Inc. Tender was disappointed that Vicky was training in my black-belt class. Vicky had had several years of training at the orphanage, just like I had, and by the end of class she was awarded a black belt. After class, everyone went home to freshen up, then David started on the lawn, while Tender and Vicky helped me with the housework. David finished first, but could not understand how we could sing while we were working. Once David finished the lawn he went ahead to freshen up.

Finally, it was dinner time and we picked up Grandma Hines and Skippy and headed to Tender's favorite hamburger place for a fun meal. This was Vicky's first time, so she ordered the same meal as Tender. The special prize was a small bag of flower seeds with instructions. David always gets two of their super burger meals. I always get a cheeseburger meal. After dinner, we headed to the park, since the weather was beautiful. Everyone was enjoying themselves. Grandma Hines and I were sitting on a park bench. Tender and Vicky were playing with Skippy. David was skipping stones over the nearby lake.

Then, out of nowhere, a man came running past at full speed and grabbed Tender. She screamed, and Skippy bit the man on the leg and held on. When Vicky saw what was happening, she jumped into the air and planted her foot on his throat. He fell to the ground, just as David came flying over and pinned him down. I ran to a phone and called the police, and they in turn called the ambulance. The ambulance and the police arrived at about the same time. Vicky had crushed the man's windpipe.

Tender informed the attendant, "He has a bronchial rupture, he is coughing up blood, and he has bubbles of air. You need to help his breathing in order to save his life." The attendant performed the procedure and rushed him to the hospital with a police escort.

Minutes later, the FBI was on the scene.

"Hi, David, is Tender okay?" asked Agent Lisa O'Brien.

"Yes, thanks to her sister, Vicky, who took out the perpetrator. He is on his way to the operating room now," David replied with a scowl.

"Which hospital are they taking him to?" she asked.

"I think Bismarck General," he replied.

Agent O'Brien got on her two-way radio and radioed ahead. "We are keeping him under FBI arrest and then surveillance until we find out who is after Tender," she assured us.

"Thank you," he nodded. They shook hands. As I turned around, Big John was on the scene. Tender was hugging him.

"Glad to see you, Big John," I said.

"Elaine, I am starting to get concerned. Tender is being stalked by someone is determined to capture and hurt her," said Big John.

"We thought this was all behind us," I said anxiously.

"From now on, Tender doesn't go anywhere without me by her side until we find out who is behind this," Big John demanded.

"I agree. We will set you up in Vicky's room; she sleeps in Tender's room every night anyway. She is having trouble sleeping alone, as she has always slept with so many roommates," I explained. Then we all headed home, dropping off Grandma Hines and Skippy, the hero dog, first.

"See you tomorrow, Grandma Hines," called Tender. Big John was coming home with us, as he was determined not to leave Tender's side.

When we got home, there was a special delivery package and a delivery worker waiting for me. I signed for the package, and gave the delivery person a tip. He was very grateful. He handed me a note and said, "God be with you. Read the note before you enter the house," he whispered. The note gave us an address to a safe house, located in Pick City, North Dakota on Lake Sakakawea and instructed us to leave everything behind.

"Please do not enter your house. Read the letter inside the envelope first," the delivery person warned us.

"What's your name?" David asked.

"Please don't enter; just leave right away." As he was leaving on his bicycle, Mary and Richard arrived too. I stopped them and told them to wait and not to enter the house. My heart was pounding as everyone around me was very confused and talking all at once. I opened the package and started to read the enclosed letter in the box. I asked Tender to sign for Vicky.

Dear Elaine and David Purdy, I am the attorney who represents Tender and Vicky's benefactor. What I am about to tell you must be read aloud to everyone on this list. If there is any person present not on the list, please have them leave. David, Elaine, Tender, Vicky, John Riley, Mary, and Richard Harris may all stay. If anyone is missing, please wait to read the letter at another time.

This will be a shock to some of you, but it won't be a shock to Tender. Tender's first mom ran away from the orphanage at age thirteen. She met a young man named Eugene Master; a cult leader from Texas who thinks he is a god. She fell in love with him, and he took advantage of her. She was with child when she realized she had made a mistake. She managed to escape, and had the baby several months later. She found a safe haven at Saint Paul's School for Girls, in Lincoln, North Dakota. Elaine, you were about eleven years old at the time. You never met Vicky's mother, but you might have seen her in the mother's ward. Ten years later she had another baby girl on August 3., That girl was Tender. This is why Tender was so determined to find Vicky. Tender knew Vicky was her half-sister.

We all stared in shock!

"Mom and Dad please let me explain. A short while ago while working on the case of the 60 missing girls I received a letter that Vicky was my sister and was in trouble. I was told not to tell anyone about Vicky until the timing was right." Tender was shaking as she spoke.

I went over and gave her a hug, "Tender why didn't you just tell us?" asked David.

"I had to put the other girls first, and if you knew you might have pursued Vicky first." Tender said, still upset. "Mom did you ever meet my first mother?"

"I never met your mother, because if a girl was pregnant she was kept in a specific area separated from us. There were always girls in that area at any given time, and we were never allowed to mingle with them, but we would go and sneak a peek. So, I am sure I have seen your birth mother," I said to Tender and Vicky. "Now I will read on." Tender seemed better and continued to sign for Vicky.

146

Now you need to know about Vicky's father. He is a very bad person. Eugene Master did not die in the ambush at the commune. He knew about the upcoming raid and left the day before, but he kept several men with him. His plan was to kidnap Tender because he felt like she was his stepdaughter and Vicky having a sister would keep both of them happy. They are not going after Vicky, since she can fight back but she would return to help Tender. But I assure you that if Vicky had not been able to stop that kidnapper, we had a sniper ready to stop him permanently.

Let me tell you about this FBI safe house. It is a fortress surrounded by an electric fence. It is also protected by guard dogs who can identify anyone wearing a bracelet. These are enclosed in the package. Please have everyone wear the bracelets, which will send a sound to the dogs that you are friendly and need to be protected. This is a requirement.

I know this is a lot to take in, but in order for the FBI to keep Tender protected, they need you to be in the safe house. The safe house is fully alarmed. The windows are bulletproof, and there is a safe room for everyone in the family. May God bless you all.

I looked through the box and handed out the bracelets to everyone on the list. Every bracelet had a name on it. No one said a word, as we were all in shock. We all got back in our cars, which now had a map along with directions to the safe house on the front seat. We drove for an hour and fifteen minutes to the location.

As we pulled up to the gate, it automatically opened and then closed behind us. A short way down the driveway there was another gate, which opened for us. Then we saw four large dogs approach the cars. After the dogs sniffed us and heard our bracelets, we were allowed to continue. As we came around the corner, we saw the most beautiful house. It was white like a southern colonial, with six large white columns. The front doors were double doors, and when I rang the doorbell, Special Agent Sisson answered the door and let us in. Suddenly, we all relaxed a little. Everyone started to talk at the same time. Then David yelled, "Quiet!"

Everyone quieted down immediately.

"Agent Sisson, can you please explain what is going on?" demanded David.

"Eugene Master was obsessed with Tender and Vicky's mother, because she got away from him. He spent years trying to find her, but he never did find her before she died. We know Vicky looks just like her mom. And since her mom passed away he is determined to get her back.

We have over twenty agents guarding this premises, as well as four guard dogs. We also have an undercover FBI agent planted amongst their crew. They have seven well-trained men ready to capture Tender. They are going to strike tonight, as our FBI spy has them believing Grandma and Grandpa Purdy are having a thirtieth anniversary party tonight at a private VFW hall nearby," Agent Sisson reported.

"Make sure you have a fake family that looks like us enter the party at the front entrance, or they will not proceed," Tender put in.

"We have one ready, made up of FBI agents, but we don't know how to imitate you, as we don't want to put any children in danger," Agent Sisson said, nodding at Tender.

"You can borrow a small child sized mannequin from a store. They will have them in any children's clothing department. Have the fake mom and dad holding the mannequin's hands. To block their view, have the fake grandma and grandpa walk behind me so they can't see that *my* legs aren't moving," Tender instructed.

"Good idea," Agent Sisson said approvingly.

Now we had to wait. We Purdys love to pass the

time by playing women against men in a friendly game. The men recruited several of the male FBI agents, and of course all the women agents joined the ladies. We played for hours, and the men were able to pull off a few wins.

"I guess it is true that girls are smarter than the boys, no matter what age we are," I teased.

Suddenly, we heard noise over the FBI two-way radio: "The suspects are on the move."

"Everyone get in position and enter the hall?" Agent Sisson said..

"No. Stop all movement, and function as if some-one is sick" Tender yelled suddenly. "Send someone to the basement. I believe they have planted a bomb in the floor joist, most likely in the middle," Tender said, acting on a gut feeling.

In minutes, they radioed back: "Fireworks found! What next?"

"How should we proceed?" Agent Sisson relayed to Tender.

"Describe 'the fireworks,' and leave nothing out," Tender demanded. By this time, she and Agent Sisson were sharing the two-way radio.

"Okay, the package is the size of a shoe box. The mud is tan, with a projectile sticking out. There is a blinking red light clock. The wires are red, green, blue, and yellow."

"Which wire is connected to the projectile, and what is the time on the clock?" asked Tender.

"Blue, and 14 minutes and 30 seconds," the agent on the radio responded.

"Which wires are connected to the clock?" asked Tender next.

"Red and yellow," came the response.

"Which two wires are connected to the battery?" Tender continued.

"Green and red," was the nervous response.

"Okay the explosive is C4. Cut the yellow wire and be careful when removing the device. Put it in the bomb-proof container," Tender said clearly.

"Are you sure it's yellow?" the agent demanded anxiously.

"Yes, don't be afraid. This is a simple device to disarm," Tender replied soothingly.

We heard a deep breath, and then a sigh of relief as the device was disarmed and put in the container for safety.

"Thank you, Tender. I think I need to change my clothes," said the agent weakly.

Inside the hall, music was playing, but the wooden shutters were closed, hiding the fact that no one was dancing. There were about ten small tables set up with four agents at each table. There was also an eight-foot guest-of-honor table at the front.

Then major trouble broke out, as Eugene Master and his men burst in and began shooting into the air (since he did not want to shoot his daughter). He thought that no one would have a gun, so just the sound of guns going off would give him control of the situation. However, once they entered the building, the FBI agents flipped their tables to the side and demanded they drop their guns and surrender.

Eugene Master yelled, and his men all started to fire their automatic rifles. However, the fight only lasted five minutes, as they were outmanned and surrounded on all sides.

Two agents were shot, but the wounds were not life-threatening. The FBI had ambulances about a mile away, hidden on a dirt road. They were there in a few minutes. After they transported the agents to a hospital, the remaining attendant declared the seven cult members unresponsive, waiting for the coroner to declare them deceased. Eugene Master was among the seven.

"Dad let's go to the hospital. I need to thank those brave agents who were willing to take a bullet for Vicky and me," Tender asked.

"Big John, what do you think?" I asked.

"Well, the threat has been contained, so I don't see why not. Also, the FBI and police have a code of conduct; if one of our agents ends up in a hospital, we all show up," Big John agreed. So, we all headed to the nearby hospital.

"Tender, this was the scariest day of my life," said Richard, wide-eyed.

"David, is there something wrong with me? I found this thrilling," said Mary. Her cheeks were flushed with excitement.

"Mary, you are a lot like me. I also find these experiences exciting, but we must always remember that seven misguided men lost their lives today. For that, I am sad," said David gently.

I noticed that Vicky was very quiet. "Vicky, we are all very sad that you lost your birth father today," I signed comfortingly. Tender hugged her sister.

Vicky shook her head. "He was never a father to me. David is my father, you are my mother, and Tender is the best sister a girl could ask for," signed Vicky.

"I have a hard time feeling sorry for these bad men after what I have seen them do to all those innocent girls. They will stand trial, this day, before the God of heaven for their sins," Vicky continued signing, a hard expression on her face.

When we entered the hospital, there must have been fifty agents present. Before we knew what was happening, an agent came up to Tender and hugged her hard. Big John yelled, "Back off, boy!" and pried Tender from the arms of the agent..

"Tender Purdy, I love you," the agent said breathlessly.

"What's this is all about?" demanded Big John angrily.

"I'm sorry. My name is Agent Bob Schneider, and under the instruction of the smartest girl on this planet, I was the one who disarmed the bomb. I now call her Tender Mercy," Agent Bob smiled.

Tender jumped into his arms for another hug and said, "You were very brave, Agent Schneider" she smiled back at him.

"Did you really know how to disarm that bomb or were you just guessing?" Agent Bob asked.

"I have studied hundreds of bomb diagrams, and I have them all memorized, just in case. That was a time-sensitive bomb, and if you had cut the wrong wire, then it would have escalated the time and would have exploded," explained Tender.

"So, you mean I had nothing to worry about?" asked Bob.

"Nothing at all," Tender smiled.

David and I just looked at each other. Then David shrugged his shoulders and folded his hands behind his head.

"That's our girl," I said proudly.

The agents cleared a path for Tender to get to the room where the wounded agents were waiting for an operating room opening. Tender came up to them.

"Agent O'Brien, thank you for being willing to help me twice and for taking a bullet for my sister. How are you feeling?" Tender asked.

"Hopefully, I will feel better soon. I was shot in the shoulder, and I would gladly take a bullet for any of the Purdys," Agent O'Brien said sincerely.

Tender went over and kissed her hand.

"Thank you," signed Vicky, with tears in her eyes.

Then Tender and Vicky went over to the other wounded agent. Tender was surprised, as she had never seen him before. She said to him, "My name is Tender. Thank you for what you did today."

"Tender, my name is Damien Fletcher. I was shot by friendly fire, as I was the spy who infiltrated Eugene Master's men. I was not supposed to be shot, but Eugene would not allow me to wear the red bandanna, which was my secret identification for agents not to shoot me. So, all I could do was drop to the floor when the shooting started," he explained.

"So where did you get shot?" Tender asked.

"Right in the bottom of the foot, but I would have

been willing to give my life for you," Agent Damien said, smiling at her.

Tender went over and hugged him while he was lying on his stomach. She said, "Thank you, Agent Damien, I love you."

Then Tender smiled at all the agents and said, "I want to thank all of you for taking on such a dangerous assignment and for keeping my family safe. May God bless my FBI family."

Finally, we headed home. We were all wound up from the excitement of the day, but we knew we needed to get some sleep since tomorrow was Big John's celebration. We all overslept on Sunday morning, and we had to rush to pick up Grandma Hines and Skippy on time.

"Tender, my dear, your face looks much better. How are you feeling?" asked Grandma Hines, examining Tender's face gently.

"Very good. I am all healed except for the black eye," Tender replied, pointing to her still-bruised eye.

The Eveready Diner was packed this morning. Everyone wanted to meet the girl who had stopped the kidnapper from taking both girls. Newspaper reporters and neighbors surrounded Vicky and bombarded her with questions. Vicky signed her answers as Tender and I interpreted. This went on for several minutes, until I finally had to stop the reporters or we would have been late to church.

When we entered our church, the same thing happened. Once again, Tender signed for this week's hero, Vicky. Vicky could not understand why there was such a fuss over her, since she had just been watching out for her sister.

After church, we were all happy to be heading off to lunch. We made up a pretense for Big John to caravan with us, since we were taking him to the country club.

"Big John, thank you for keeping Vicky from getting crushed by all those admirers!" I said, getting in the car.

"It was my pleasure. Now I have two girls to protect," he said. We agreed that Big John would follow us in his car. We had a delay tactic in place so as not to get to the country club before the rest of the guests.

"Elaine, my dear, could you stop off at my place before we go? I forgot something," said Grandma Hines, winking at me. When we arrived at her house, Tender took her keys and retrieved a bag containing a present for Big John.

As we approached the Bismarck Country Club, there was no way Big John would expect a surprise party for himself. There were always so many cars in the parking lot, he would never notice that there were more than usual today. As we entered the room, he said, "This is a very large room just for one family"

Then everyone jumped out and started to sing, "For he's a jolly good fellow!"

Big John looked up and saw the banner: "Congratulations, Special Agent John Riley" Director Lance and Chief Purdy came up to the microphone. I interpreted in sign language so Vicky could understand.

"We are here today to honor Special Agent Big John (as everyone likes to call you). Congratulations, Big John. I am pleased to announce that the Secretary of Defense has approved your transfer to the Bismarck Police Force, as a liaison with the FBI. This means you are on loan and must obey all the orders from the chief of the Bismarck Police Department, no matter who that may be," announced Director Lance.

Chief Purdy stepped to the microphone and said, "Would Tender please step forward?"

Tender came forward, holding a Bible with both hands, Big John put his hand on it, with tears in his eyes he repeated the oath after Chief Purdy:

I, John Riley, do solemnly swear to defend and protect the Constitution of the United States of America and the Constitution of the great state of North Dakota against enemies, foreign and domestic, so help me God.

Everyone in the room clapped and cheered, because they all loved Big John. Big John picked up his favorite girl, Tender, and gave her a bear hug. As they all sat down, the social worker handling Vicky adoption papers stepped forward, along with Big John

"This very important lady is Johann Gallo. Now I need David, Elaine, Tender, and Vicky to please come forward." Big John told Mrs. Gallo to proceed.

"Although adoptions usually takes at least one year to finalize, by order of Governor William L. Guy, as of today, Vicky Smith will now be known as Vicky Purdy. Mr. And Mrs. Purdy, here is the birth certificate for your newly adopted daughter, Vicky Purdy," Johann smiled.

We all hugged, and the place exploded with cheering and clapping. Skippy joined in with excited barking; I guess even Skippy approved.

David and I had noticed that ever since the attack on Tender, Vicky always held Tender's hand, no matter where they went. I guess it is true that big sister always watches out for little sister.

After a wonderful afternoon of celebrating, we headed back home, dropping off Grandma Hines and Skippy on the way. We were all excited to get back to work on cases again, especially Richard and Mary. We all headed into the living room, and David stood up to announce the agenda for next week. I had decided I would be the interpreter until everyone learned sign language.

"Well, first I need Richard and Mary to go back out for a few minutes," David instructed. Richard and Mary gave him puzzled looks, but they promptly went back out.

After Richard and Mary had left the room, David continued. "Richard and Mary will be going to their prom on Friday, and the following week they will graduate high school. I recommend we hire them as full-time employees, at a salary of $100 a week each. We will now take a vote." David listed our names and took down our votes as we spoke.

Big John, Tender and I all voted 'yes'.

"Vicky?"

"I vote "yes." And I love my new name," Vicky signed, smiling. Then we brought Richard and Mary back into the room.

"Richard and Mary, we have voted to invite you to be employed full-time on the Purdy team, if you are interested as soon as you graduate from high school. Please let us know by next Saturday if you are interested," said David, smiling at them both.

"We don't need to wait until next Saturday to give my answer. We have both been praying that you would ask us to be on the team full time. My answer is 'yes,' exclaimed Richard, jumping out of his seat and pumping his fist in the air.

"I never thought I would love police work, but I do. My answer is yes, too," said Mary, smiling, although she stayed seated. "Richard and I have decided we want to join the Bismarck police force," Mary explained.

"Then you two need to step up your karate lessons to three times a week, as you will only have one year to prepare for the next state police training," I smiled.

"That's a good plan." Mary nodded.

"Wait a minute—what will our salary be?" asked Richard, sitting back down.

"Tender, what do you think they are worth?" I asked, teasing.

"I was thinking maybe 50 cents per hour," said Tender, joining in the joke.

"Tender, come on; let's give them at least.75 cents per hour," Big John said, with a wink at me.

"Now you listen here! We want at least $1.25 per hour," Mary shouted. I could see her face getting red.

David jumped in before things got out of hand.

"Okay, okay! We agreed we will give you each $100 a week," David said soothingly.

This time, both Richard and Mary jumped into the air with excitement.

"If it wasn't for you two, we would not have found out about those other missing girls. We have seen how valuable you two are to Team Purdy. You will be our full-time investigators this summer," David continued. This pleased Richard and Mary, as they grinned at each other and then sat back down.

"Next on the agenda: Big John, would you please go out for a minute?" David asked.

When Big John had left the room, David continued, "Okay, now this is a big request." He took out a set of blueprints and laid them on the coffee table. "We want to construct an apartment for Big John, on the back of our house. We want Big John to be comfortable, so I have asked cousin Alex, who is a contractor, to draw up these plans. We will build one bedroom, one full bath, a galley kitchen no more than twelve feet in total length, and a small living and dining room. It includes a 12 x 12 utility and storage area for laundry." David said, pointing out the various features on the blueprints. Then he called for a vote. The vote was unanimous.

Now that we had unanimous votes, we asked Big John to come back in.

"What happened to going out for only one minute?" Big John grumbled as he came in with his arms crossed.

"Well, Big John, I think you will be happy we took our time," David said, amused.

Big John looked down at the blueprints and asked, "What are these blueprints for?"

"This will be your new apartment if you want it. It will be attached to the back of the house, so you will always be close by to protect Vicky and me," said Tender, putting her hand on Big John's arm.

"No way! That is beautiful," Big John cried, as he put both his hands over his mouth. Then we all received a Big John hug, which always takes your breath away. "Ever since my wife died, and my children have grown up and moved out, I have felt so lonely rattling around in my apartment all by myself. I love you guys; thank you for making me part of your family. Since Tender, and now Vicky is in my life, I love them like they were my very own daughters who I need to watch out for. I definitely want it!" Big John smiled through his tears.

"Alex is going to apply for the permits this week, and the construction will take about ninety days to complete. Meanwhile, you should give your landlord your notice," David suggested. Big John wanted to give us another hug, but everyone passed.

"Is that what it's going to be like living around here?" Big John joked. We all laughed, as Tender said, "Not with me" and gave Big John another hug. "See, that's why I love Tender the most," Big John laughed.

On Monday, Tender went back to school, and Vicky was scheduled to be evaluated to see where she would fit in at Tender's school. David, Big John, and I met with Chief Purdy to discuss the rules regarding what Big John was allowed to do on behalf of the Bismarck police department. Everything was quiet for the rest of the week. We were all excited about Mary and Richard's prom, and on Friday night David went and picked up Mrs. Hines and Skippy. Every family member, including Big John, Grandma Hines, and Skippy, all came to Grandma and Grandpa Purdy's house to see Mary in her gown. Richard came to the door in his tux, looking so handsome. Mary came downstairs, so beautiful in her form-fitting, strapless, gold sequin dress. She looked comfortable and confident, and the dress matched her shiny blonde hair and sunny smile. Richard was speechless; Mary was a tomboy and had never dressed up much, but today she looked spectacular.

David went over to Richard and gave him the keys to the Mercedes. "Richard, I just had it detailed today—and good luck with the other thing," whispered David in his ear.

"Thank you, because I think I am going to throw up," Richard whispered back fearfully.

The entire family gave both Richard and Mary a hug and a kiss, and they were on their way.

"I advise everyone to hang around; it might be worth it," David said mysteriously. So, we ordered pizza and played games till everyone fell asleep except David.

Finally, at 1:30 AM, Mary and Richard waltzed giddily back through the door. I heard voices and woke up to see Mary, radiant with love. I ran and woke Tender and Vicky. As we came into the room Mary immediately held up her left hand for us all to see the beautiful new engagement ring sparkling there!

"Mary, tell me everything!" squealed Tender.

Mary exclaimed, "Richard had it all planned! We were dancing in the middle of the floor, and just as the dance ended, he knelt on one knee, and said, 'Mary Purdy, I have never loved anyone like I do you. Will you be my wife?' So, I said, 'Yes, Richard Harris, I would be honored to be your wife.' Everyone at the dance cheered for us, except Richard's old girlfriend. She just huffed loudly and stomped off, taking off his old school ring, which she had never returned, and threw it across the room." One of his friends retrieved it and with a smile handed it back to him.

Richard pulled the old ring out of his pocket and showed it to us. We all congratulated them with big hugs.

Finally, we all headed home. On the way, I told David how upset I was with him.

"David, how could you not tell your wife it was going to be tonight? I am so angry at you." I said, punching his arm.

"I didn't tell you about the surprise because I promised Richard to keep it a secret." David protested. I understood that David would never break a promise, but I was still not happy that I hadn't been told it was tonight."

Over the next few weeks, things seemed to get back to normal. Richard and Mary graduated from high school. Tender was reading college books on accounting, because she wanted to get her CPA within one year, and since school was out for the summer, she was bored. She also continued studying medical journals. She was not interested in going to medical school, but she liked knowing how to diagnose any symptoms that might come her way. Vicky took the SAT and received a score of 1520, almost as good as Tender.

Tender made a list of all the guests she wanted the FBI to invite to the annual awards ceremony. Tender had invitations sent to Vicky, Grandpa and Grandma Purdy, Grandma Hines, David, me, Richard and Mary, Uncle Frank, and other family members, including her cousin Anne and family. Since Big John was an agent, he already had an invitation and since we were over the number of guest allowed, Big John let us use his allotment of guest.

On the day of the ceremony, we girls got our hair done, as well as getting a manicure and pedicure. We had also purchased new outfits for the ceremony a few weeks ago, and they were ready for pickup. David, Grandpa, Big John, and Richard had all purchased new suits, and they went together to pick them up.

David got ready first, because Vicky, Tender, and I wanted to surprise him when we came down the hall all dressed up. He kept yelling, "Come on. We are going to be late."

All three of us came in wearing the same dress. They were red with white lace and a white belt. Our hair was done up, and we all had the same style of red shoes. David put his hand over his mouth as he watched us come down the hall together.

"Wow! I have never seen three more beautiful ladies than you three." he exclaimed.

The awards ceremony was held at the Bismarck Country Club. As we tried to enter, we were surprised that the double doors were shut. Then the maître d' opened the doors and announced Miss Tender Purdy and her guests.

An usher escorted us to two round tables next to each other. We were privileged to be sitting with Agent Sisson and his wife. Our table was very close to the head table. At the table next to us were all of Tender's invited guests. Tender demanded that Big John sit at our table.

Mrs. Sisson whispered in Tender's ear, "Thank you, Tender, for saving our marriage." Tender just smiled. It took about another hour for everyone to arrive. Director Lance introduced Tender to J. Edgar Hoover.

"Miss Purdy, I have been hearing some wonderful things about you" remarked Mr. Hoover. "Can you tell me something about myself?"

Tender looked at him for a short time and then started speaking.

"You were the first director of the FBI. Born on January 1, 1895, you are 5-feet-7-inches tall. You went to George Washington University, and you became a lawyer in 1916. You are left-handed. You started the FBI on May 10, 1924, with the help of Theodore Roosevelt and President Calvin Coolidge. You own a lot of dogs. You play golf. In 1931, you sent Al Capone to Alcatraz because he was the head of the Chicago gangs. Oh, and those are not your shoes, and your feet are in pain, as the shoes are too small."

"That is amazing. How old are you?" exclaimed Mr. Hoover.

"Five years old," Tender smiled.

He just shook his head in amazement and said, "Young lady, you are 100 percent correct; my feet are killing me." We all laughed sympathetically.

The food was delicious, but I could tell by the way Tender played with it that she would have preferred a cheeseburger and fries.

During the ceremony, outstanding agents from across the country received different awards. Our own Agent Sisson got an award for completing cases in the shortest time.

Finally, J. Edgar Hoover came to the podium. "And now, ladies and gentlemen, this highest award goes to the agent who has solved at least two cases, concerning one of the top ten most wanted criminals in the United States. This award goes to Agent Tender Purdy."

David and I almost fell off our chairs.

Tender got up like it was nothing and received her award, smiling and waving at the cheering audience.

Director Lance also handed her an envelope and said, "This is in appreciation for all your help." Then she sat down and handed me the award and the envelope. Every agent attending the banquet came by our table to congratulate her. But the person most proud of her was her sister, Vicky.

Before we left, Director Lance asked for a private meeting with Team Purdy. We were escorted along with Agent Sisson to a room across the hall. We were all asked to sit down at a table that was set up with, notepads and pencils.

NINE

Top Secret Case

"**W**hat I am about to tell you is of national security and must not leave this room. Please understand that if this information is leaked, the person responsible could spend up to five years in a military prison," Director Lance said seriously. Then he asked everyone on Team Purdy to promise confidentiality. We all agreed not to speak a word to anyone. We were also not to discuss the matter even with other agents unless they were already briefed. I was not concerned about Tender, as she never tells a secret when asked not to. I also knew that David would never break a promise. Mary would try to keep control of Richard, and Big John would go to the grave keeping secrets.

Once Director Lance had all our promises, he took a deep breath before starting. First, he pointed to the door, indicating to Special Agent Sisson to make sure that two agents are posted at the door; they were instructed not to let anyone in, regardless of the reason. Then he spoke.

"Two days ago, Captain Peter Johansson, the son of Secretary of the Navy, Cornelius Johansson, was charged as a traitor to the United States of America. The penalty for this crime is death. He is being accused of selling a F-100 Super Sabre jet to the Russians. First thing on Monday, you are to report to my office for instructions on how to proceed. Meanwhile, Tender, here are the books you will need to familiarize yourself with military law. Eventually we will all fly to Washington DC."

Director Lance dismissed us, stressing again the confidential nature of the case. Then we all made our way out of the country club and headed home.

On our way home, I opened the envelope to see what Tender had received for being the FBI agent of the year. Inside the envelope were eight seven-day passes to a large amusement park in California, as well as a voucher for the use of the FBI jet. The FBI cabin in the woods was also reserved for us for seven days and six nights.

Tender was so excited. We started to discuss who she wanted to take with her to the amusement park. She replied that she wanted to take her cousin Anne.

The next day, we decided that we would vacation in California after completing the case we had just received. We were not sure how long the case would take, but we wanted to plan our trip for the middle of July, providing we completed the case. I spoke to the FBI coordinator and requested the use of the cabin for the third week of July, if the jet would accommodate the dates we chose. She informed us that it would be reserved.

The following day David went by the police station and informed Chief Purdy that we would be away for undetermined leave. He was not pleased and denied our request until he spoke to Director Lance. I waited in my office until the chief called David in.

"David, I have spoken to Director Lance and after he informed me of the situation, I have agreed, for interest of the country. You have my blessing."

"Thank you, sir." David said, Then the chief took hold of David's hand and squeezed it as hard as he could, pulled him close and whispered in his ear. "Please save this young solider from the death penalty."

"That's our plan." David whispered back.

The next few weeks would be the most difficult and challenging our team ever faced. Tender started reviewing the twelve books Director Lance had given her. School was in summer recess for the next ten weeks, and Tender was excited about learning about military laws. They were very different but not very complicated she told us. However, the mystery of the missing F-100 jet would be a challenge for Team Purdy.

Sunday did not go as it normally did, as Tender never left her room except to eat. She was not willing to take even a little time to play with Skippy. Every hour on the hour, I checked in on her. By the end of the day, when I checked in on her, she was sound asleep at her desk. I picked her up, changed her into her night clothes, and tucked her into her bed. Her books were all over the bed, floor, and desk. I tried to tidy them up, but I was concerned I was putting them in the wrong place.

Monday came and the team met at headquarters. Director Lance gave us military badges that we would need to enter the courtroom as well as the Maryland Military Base. The instructions were different for both the courtroom and while we were on the base. We would be accompanied by several Secret Service agents, who had several vehicles awaiting our arrival. Then we were off to the airport and onto the plane. Tender was surprised that there were Secret Service agents on the plane, since they usually guard the President of the United States.

Big John knew most of the agents, and they saluted him and addressed him as Agent John Riley. They were very serious and never engaged Big John, not even with a handshake. Big John told us later they are all business and trained not to be distracted. Big John also told me they were here to protect Tender, since he, himself, had once been on the Secret Service and had protected many of the presidents. Once on board, Tender's favorite flight attendant, Agent Carrie Jackson, had breakfast ready for the whole crew. Agent Clifford Gregory was our pilot.

"What is the weather report for today's flight?" Richard asked with fear in his eyes. He told us earlier that he was afraid of flying.

"Not good. We will be flying through a hurricane at 33,000 feet," Agent Clifford smiled.

"What?" Richard said in a squeaky voice.

Mary slapped his arm. "He is only kidding." she said, shaking her head. We all laughed.

"It's so easy to trick Richard," I thought to myself. Once we were in the air, Richard had a lot of questions.

"Tender is a military lawyer like a regular lawyer? Does a military lawyer go to law school?" asked Richard.

"Military laws are vastly different. A military judge oversees the trial. The lawyers are military officers. In the military they are called JAG officers. In 1948, the United States Air Force founded the Judge Advocate General school. JAG officers are trained in military conduct and laws. This form of justice is extremely strict and has very little allowance for leniency," Tender said. "If you commit a crime that requires the death penalty and are found guilty, then you will be put to death."

"Tender, can you explain in more detail please?" asked Mary curiously.

"If you are accused of a military crime, you are assigned a JAG officer as a lawyer, or you can hire your own civilian lawyer at your own cost."

"How do they select a jury?" asked Richard. He wanted to know as much about the process as possible.

"The commanding officer will choose the members of the jury from military men he knows, or he will interview members 'Voir Dire.'"

"What does that mean?" asked Richard.

"It means to find jury members who will be fair and objective. In a civil trial, the jury is selected after being questioned by both the prosecuting and defense attorneys, and a juror can be excused. However, once a member is chosen in a military hearing, that member cannot be excused." Tender was enjoying recalling what she had read.

"Tender, I served on a jury last year in a murder case and we had to have a unanimous verdict to convict. Does that differ from a military trial?" asked Big John. He already knew the answer, but he was enjoying hearing Tender explain the process.

"A military hearing requires a two-thirds majority to convict, except in a death penalty case like the one we are going to try. In such cases, all the members have to agree he is guilty," Tender said, looking serious.

"Tender, how many members serve on in a trial?" I asked, getting involved in the conversation.

"Eight," she replied.

Richard was still nervous about flying, and he passed Tender a note asking how many miles it was to Washington DC. She returned the note with the answer, "Still 1,343 miles, or about 3 hours." Richard groaned and put his face in his hands.

We kept the conversation going to distract Richard, and before we knew it we had landed. Several FBI vehicles were waiting to bring us to our destination. The Secret Service agents walked in front, in back, and on both sides surrounding Tender. They escorted us to a safe house, and some agents remained outside all around the building, while others went inside, following Tender around everywhere she went. The odd thing was that they never talked, and no matter what question Tender asked she only received a nod, never an answer. A few times, if she was about to walk in front of a window, they would say to wait; they would look behind the blinds, and then give her a sign to proceed.

The safe house was different than the previous safe houses we had been in. Tender noted, "This house looks similar to the Frank Lloyd Wright house called the Westcott House, built in 1908 in Springfield, Ohio."

"Tender, this is a strange-looking house; was this guy Frank famous?" Richard asked.

"Yes, Richard. Frank Lloyd Wright was a very famous architect." Tender closed her eyes to bring up her recall. "He was born on June 8, 1867, in Wisconsin. He designed over one thousand structures, both commercial and residential. He died on April 9, 1959, in Arizona."

Once we settled in, we were summoned to report to the conference room.

We were greeted by a tall man in a suit. "Hello Team Purdy, my name is Cornelius Johansson. As of today, I am still the Secretary of the Navy. Hi, Tender; it's nice to see you again. I am proud of Team Purdy and all the agents who assisted in rescuing the sixty missing girls. Now I need all of you to help me personally. My son, Captain Peter

Johansson, is charged with stealing an F-100 jet plane and selling it to the Russians. The evidence against him is so strong, I almost believe he is guilty." With tears in his eyes, he walked over to Tender and took her hand. "But my heart tells me he is innocent," he finished.

As he fell to his knees in tears, Mrs. Johansson came over to comfort him. She just looked at Tender and whispered, "Please help us."

Tender, David, and I, along with Director Lance, went to the front of the room, where three podiums were set up. Tender climbed the two steps to her podium. One podium was for Director Lance, and the third podium was for JAG officer Lieutenant Linda Kincaid.

"Director Lance, who is the civilian attorney I will be working with?" Lieutenant Kincaid asked.

"Right next to you. This is Tender Purdy," Director Lance replied, pointing to Tender.

"You have got to be kidding me. I need an experienced attorney! Is this a joke?" Lieutenant Kincaid demanded. She looked furious.

Just then, Secretary Johansson came forward, overhearing her remarks. "Lieutenant, Tender Purdy is more than competent to help you, and I will put my son's life in her hands," he said sternly, putting his hand on Tender's shoulder.

"Yes sir, but she can't be more than five or six years old! Please stop and reconsider your decision, or your son may die," the lieutenant protested.

I stepped in. "Lieutenant Kincaid, I assure you that Tender is a very good Bar certified attorney, although she can't be first chair, she will be able to help you find their son not guilty." I was used to people not believing in Tender's abilities, but the lieutenant's attitude was making me angry.

"That may be so, but military justice is very different than civil court. I will have no part in this, nor will I be blamed for Captain Johansson death." Lieutenant Kincaid packed her things and started to leave.

"Please, stop." Tender called after her. Lieutenant Kincaid turned around to look at Tender. "Since you are leaving, please answer a few questions." The lieutenant folded her arms and gave Tender a nasty look. "Did you complete the Article 32 proceedings?" Tender asked with a smile.

"What do you know about Article 32, young lady?" she replied, still with her arms crossed, but now looking curiously at Tender.

"Well, I know it is the uniform code to decide whether the charges are dismissed or whether we will go before the military judge for trial," replied Tender.

"Wait a minute; how could you know that?" she questioned.

"Also, has the commanding office chosen the eight members of the jury yet?" Tender now folded her arms and gave the lieutenant her most intense look.

"Wait a minute. I know what is going on; you have an earpiece, and someone is feeding you questions. You must think I am stupid." She shook her head indignantly and started to walk out again.

Tender yelled after her. "I understand you are afraid; it took you seven years of school to get where you are, and for the last three years you have been just a runner for all the male JAG officers. This is your first real case, and your commanding officer is constantly telling you that you are not ready. But if you leave, he will treat you as a quitter, and he will never give you another case," Tender said, unfolding her arms.

Lieutenant Kincaid put her hands over her face and shuddered. I went over and gave her a hug. I whispered in her ear, "Trust Tender. She can do this."

"Very well, you are right; I must finish this case. I am the first woman JAG officer, and I need to succeed." She gave Tender a weak smile.

"Okay, let's get our team working. Lieutenant

Kincaid, we have our passes to enter the base, but the Secret Service agents protecting Tender need theirs." I said.

Lieutenant Kinkaid opened her briefcase and handed out the passes to enter the court chambers.

Just then it hit me, I whispered. "David that is the man in the meeting." I said.

"What man are you talking about?" David whispered back.

"Remember the day Tender went into Director Lance's office unannounced? That's who was in that private meeting, Secretary of the Navy Johansson." I just smiled, knowing David loved knowing.

"I could not be prouder of our daughter for not telling us when she is asked to keep a top secret." David whispered with a smile back.

"Lieutenant Kincaid, you and I need to see Captain Johansson tomorrow," Tender announced, as she looked up to see her David and I smiling. "Big John, take Dad and Richard with you, and question everyone about the events of July 3 & 4," Tender continued.

"What questions are we to ask?" Big John asked, taking notes.

"First, find out who was on duty the morning of July 4. Ask questions such as what rituals Captain Johansson always followed before he entered the cockpit and took off. Ask this question to everyone on duty that morning. Ask them if he normally has any conversation with the crew or other captains before he takes off. Does he take a snack on the plane, or a drink? I am sure every pilot has little rituals like making the sign of the cross, smoking their favorite cigar, how they carry their helmet, or at what time they put on their leather head covering. Does anyone know why they wear a helmet?" Tender asked.

Richard raised his hand first.

"Yes, Richard."

"Is the helmet so if they crash, it will protect their head." He smiled.

"Yes—actually, they wear a helmet in case they must eject from the plane and parachute down. The helmet protects their head from injury," Tender explained.

"Mom and Mary, you are to discover what Captain Johansson is like off base. Go to his apartment, close your eyes, and let your sense of smell take over. Ask any neighbors if they smelled a funny odor coming from his apartment or unusual noise on July 3 or 4," Tender said.

"What smells should we be looking for?" asked Mary, sniffing experimentally.

"Chloroform or anesthesia. It should smell like

a hospital room," Tender added. Lieutenant Kincaid gave them the key and the address, along with directions to Captain Johansson's apartment.

TEN

Treason and Court-Martial

T he following morning, Director Lance and the Secret Service agents guarding Tender headed to the air force base and met up with JAG officer Kincaid. She was surprised that Tender had so many bodyguards.

"Is this necessary? We are on a military base," she said, furrowing her eyebrows.

Director Lance looked her in the eye and said, "This little girl is very important to the FBI and to this country. There have already been several attempts in which bad people tried to injure her, or even worse." He folded his arms over his chest and glared.

"Really? Gosh, Tender, I am so sorry. I am sorry, too, for the way I conducted myself yesterday," she said, bending down to talk to Tender.

"I understand. You have taken a stand for women, and the only reason you were on this case is that none of your male JAG officers wanted it. They believe you have no chance of winning, but they might be disappointed," Tender smiled at Lieutenant Kincaid.

We were brought into a small room with a table and metal chairs with poor lighting. I requested a flashlight and magnifying glass, and they were issued to us. Director Lance was also allowed in, but he was not allowed to speak, as we were being monitored for sight and sound.

When Captain Johansson entered the room, he was limping. Just like everyone who meets Tender for the first time, he was surprised. However, when Tender and Director Lance were introduced by officer Kincaid, Captain Johansson didn't seem to care. Tender asked to see his arms, and then she turned her back to him and asked him to remove his shirt and dropped his pants. Lieutenant Kincaid checked him over with a magnifying glass, as Tender requested.

"Nothing," Lieutenant Kincaid reported.

"Now please remove your right sock I noticed you were limping when you entered," Tender asked. Captain Johansson did everything just as she asked. Once he removed his sock Tender noticed his right foot was black and blue with bruises.

"Tender, I don't see a puncture wound," Lieutenant Kincaid said anxiously as she thoroughly looked him over with a magnifying glass. She looked at Tender with fear in her eyes, as their whole case was based on the premise that Captain Johansson had been drugged.

Tender closed her eyes for the longest time. The captain wanted to know what she was doing. Still with her eyes closed, Tender said, "Check between his toes."

In a matter of seconds, Lieutenant Kincaid had thrown her arms around Tender and kissed her on the cheek. "You are amazing!" she exclaimed joyfully. Director Lance just stood there confused.

"Now, Captain, we know you didn't steal an F-100 fighter jet on the morning of July 4," Lieutenant Kincaid said to Captain Johansson, but smiling at Tender. "Captain, please tell us what you remember of the events of that day. Leave nothing out," she instructed. Then, she couldn't help herself; she spun around and let out a whoop.

"I'm confused; why are you so happy? I am accused of stealing an F-100 jet plane, and I am going to die for my crime," the captain said, looking perplexed.

"Please tell us what you remember of that day," she repeated, still smiling.

"I was out late that night because I was enjoying myself in the company of a beautiful woman who paid for all my drinks. We headed up to my apartment, and the next thing I knew, I was being arrested," he recalled, running his hands through his hair.

"Did she have a foreign accent?" Tender asked.

"Yes, but she told me she was from Belgium."

"So, she had a French accent," Tender pressed.

"No, it definitely wasn't French."

"We suspect it was Russian," Tender said, looking at him sternly.

"Russian? How can that be?"

"Please tell us why you think you are guilty of selling an F-100 jet," continued Tender.

"Well, I am positive I was in the cockpit flying the plane. I don't remember getting in the cockpit, but I spoke to the dispatch officer, who ordered me to return the plane. I think I landed the plane; I just don't know where I landed." He put his hands over his face in disgust.

"What happened next?" Tender asked.

"I woke up in my room, sick as a dog, on the afternoon of July 4. I was being arrested, and because of all the drinking, I vomited all that day and had a terrible headache. I was so dizzy I needed help walking until the morning of July 5."

Lieutenant Kincaid took pictures of the bottom of Captain Johansson's right foot with her polaroid camera. For the next two days, Tender and Lieutenant Kincaid, worked out a plan of action.

On the first day of the trial, we all entered the court room. Officer Kincaid went over to shake the hand of officer Kevin Martone. Martone muttered in her ear, "Save the Air Force some time and have your captain plead guilty. I will get the death penalty off the table."

"Thanks for the advice, but we will take our chances."

The court room was packed with military friends of Captain Johansson. His father and mother sat right behind him on the bench. Tender had a booster seat, but during the trial she would not be able to address the judge. Tender and Lieutenant Kincaid came up with a plan that if Tender had some insight into the case, she would tap the table three times and hand Lieutenant Kincaid an index card. The judge asked for the charges to be read.

"In the case of the United States Air Force against Captain Peter Johansson, the defendant is being charged with willfully stealing an F-100 Super Sabre jet on July 4. He is also being charged with treason for selling that same jet to the Russians," Lieutenant Martone reported.

ELEVEN

The Military Trial

"Captain Johansson, please rise. How do you plead?" the judge asked.

"Not guilty," answered Captain Johansson. He saluted the judge, who returned the salute.

"Lieutenant Martone, you may proceed with your case," the judge ordered.

"Members of the jury, thank you for your service. I want you to imagine you were the president of a large company, and one of your most trusted men stole a crucial piece of equipment. How would you feel? Angry? Disappointed in all the time you spent training this employee, only to be betrayed? If you pay taxes, that's how all Americans feel today. Just think, in the past, we would have the trial, and once the thief was found guilty, the citizens would just go out and hang him. Well, that's how I feel right now.

The Air Force will prove Captain Peter Johansson received one million dollars coming from Russia, which he deposited into an account in France. The Air Force is asking for the death penalty. Thank you." JAG officer Martone sat down.

Lieutenant Kincaid stood up to speak. "Good morning, members of the jury; I am Lieutenant Kincaid. That was amazing, Lieutenant Martone; I guess we should send someone out to the hardware store to buy some rope. Why even have the trial? The problem with the prosecution's theory is that we have evidence that will exonerate Captain Johansson. Incidentally, my co-chair is Miss Tender Purdy. Don't be fooled by her age; she is very smart," said the lieutenant, as Tender waved and smiled.

As she sat down, Tender whispered something in her ear. Lieutenant Kincaid spoke again. "Judge, may I request that when we close, my co-chair give the closing arguments?"

The judge looked over at opposing council.

"No objection from the Air Force; if the lieutenant wants to let a kindergartener do the closing arguments, that is fine with me." Martone burst out laughing, along with his co-chair.

"So be it," said the judge as he hit the gavel down so hard it cracked. Due to bad weather the judge ordered everyone to be back tomorrow morning, at 0900 hours. "We will hear from the first witness at that time. Court is adjourned."

Captain Johansson was taken away in cuffs, and we all headed to the FBI safe house to discuss what we had learned and how to proceed. When we arrived, dinner was prepared, and enjoyed by everyone, then we all headed to the conference room. Tender spoke first.

"Lieutenant Kincaid you were wonderful today." Tender smiled at her.

Richard raised his hand.

"Yes, Richard?" Tender called.

"Tender, what mistakes did the prosecution make today?" Richard asked.

"Richard, when the opposing council is over-confident instead of being humble, the members of the jury will take that into consideration when they decide the outcome of this case. This, and the fact that they did not do their due diligence. If they had, they would have discovered that a Russian woman tricked Captain Johansson into letting her into his apartment. I predict the opposing council will apologize to me in the morning for his remarks about me," Tender said confidently.

"Tender, I disagree; he is the JAG's top advocate and is under no pressure to win this case, he will never apologize although I wish he would." Lieutenant Kincaid said, shaking her head.

Mary interjected, "He sure is handsome." All the girls laughed, but not David and Richard.

"Elaine, Tender is so smart. Is she a practicing lawyer in North Dakota?" asked Lieutenant Kincaid admiringly.

"Yes, but she cannot try a case alone until she is twenty-one. I said.

Tender and the whole team discussed what evidence had been discovered that day and what was discovered in our favor. Then we got ready for bed.

Tender did not like her room; every exterior wall was glass from floor to ceiling, with no shades, so that when the sun came up, so did you. Knowing we would be here for several days, I asked Director Lance to arrange for FBI staff to put blankets up to cover the glass.

Breakfast was certainly to David's liking—a buffet with the most delicious Belgium waffles, and every breakfast food you could think of. Tender's favorite was twenty types of cereals she could choose from. I finally had to pull David away from the table, as it was time to head back to the trial.

Before the trial began, the judge called both JAG officers and Director Lance into his chambers. "I am only going to say this once: I have never been so angry as I was at the conduct of Lieutenant Martone, in your reference to Miss Purdy."

"It was only a joke, sir!"

"Well, maybe if you had done your homework, you would have discovered she is a Special Agent with the FBI, and she was agent of the year for 1964. This is not coming from me, but from the President of the United States: one more mean-spirited comment, or you will be washing dishes in the mess hall for your remaining years in the military. Is that understood?" the judge barked.

Lieutenant Martone stood up and saluted. "Yes, sir. Message received, sir." On the way out, I overheard Director Lance whisper a bad word into the ear of Lieutenant Martone.

Lieutenant Kincaid started writing in her daily logbook everything she could see and hear about her first case. She told me later that her grandfather had always told her, early on in her life, to write down everything she encountered, whether small or great, because it would help her in her life's journey. From the age of twelve, she had never missed a day.

She wrote, *"I have come to understand how those who are close to this little girl love her like their own, especially this scary Special Agent John Riley. Yesterday, I thought he was going to explode. Also, even though she is not the leader, Elaine Purdy is always keeping everyone under control. I did notice that even though David is quiet, when he gives an order, everyone obeys. I conclude that Tender and Elaine solve the problems, and David and John Riley execute the plan to a 'T'. Mary Purdy and Richard Harris do the grunt work. I only hope they can do their magic for Captain Johansson."* Lieutenant Kincaid had to stop writing, as court was about to begin.

Tender whispered in her ear, "Lieutenant, how is your logbook coming along?" The lieutenant just shook her head and smiled.

"All rise," ordered the court clerk.

As we all stood, the judge hit his gavel and announced, "Please be seated."

Just then, Lieutenant Martone stood up. "May I speak, please?" he said.

"Yes," answered the judge in a harsh voice.

"I want to apologize to Miss Tender Purdy for my uncalled-for comments yesterday. Please forgive me?" he asked as he came over and saluted Tender. She returned the salute back and gave him a smile. I think Tender loves it when she can predict how someone is going to react after making a mistake. Lieutenant Kincaid smiled too, knowing full well that Lieutenant Martone was really a nice guy.

"I would like Colonel Norman Martin to please take the stand," Lieutenant Martone directed.

"Sir, would you please state your name and rank?" questioned Lieutenant Martone.

"Colonel Norman Martin,"

"Colonel, how long have you been the commanding officer of this Air Force Base?

"Going on eleven years."

"Colonel, of those eleven years, would you say that July 4, 1965, was a bad day?"

"It was more like a nightmare " The Colonel pounded the rail in anger.

"One of my F-100 supersonic jets was missing, my best pilot was being accused of treason, and it happened on my watch," answered the Colonel, shaking his head.

"Colonel, have you ever had to reprimand or had to discipline Captain Johansson?"

"Yes, I have; many of the men under my command are under a lot of stress, and on occasion they may get a reprimand for disorderly conduct or for drunkenness. That offense would result in an Article 134 citation."

"Colonel, has Captain Johansson ever received an Article 134 citation?"

"Yes—but" the Colonel was interrupted, by Lieutenant Martone

"I have no more questions for this witness!" said Martone abruptly.

"Lieutenant Kincaid, would you like to question the Colonel?" the judge asked, nodding at Kincaid.

"Yes, Your Honor. Colonel, on how many occasions did you have to give Captain Johansson an Article 134 citation, and why?"

"Only once, and he received thirty days confinement as punishment, as he was defending the honor of a young lady. I am proud to be his commanding officer."

Just as he finished speaking, Lieutenant Martone jumped up and shouted, "I object to this statement and request it be stricken from the record!"

"Be careful counselor; the Colonel has the right to express his opinion. Now be seated," demanded the judge.

"Colonel, I have only one more question: when we interviewed you, you told me you believe Captain Johansson is not guilty?"

"Stealing a jet is almost impossible to achieve alone; it would have taken many men or women, who are willing to betray their country, as well as a lot of planning, to pull it off. So, if such a plan were being devised somehow, surely this secret would have been revealed and stopped. Nothing happens under my command that I do not know about," finished the Colonel.

"Thank you, sir. I have no more questions for the Colonel."

"Colonel, you may step down," said the judge. As the Colonel stepped down, he did something that surprised everyone in the room: he went and stood in front of Captain Johansson and saluted him. Immediately, the captain jumped up and returned the salute. Every person in that court room, including the eight members of the jury, stood and saluted the Colonel, as he is well respected by his men. It was sweet to see Tender stand and salute, along with Lieutenant Kincaid.

Finally, the judge spoke again. "Lieutenant Martone, you may call your next witness."

"Your honor, may I approach the bench?"

"Yes, you may," the judge answered, as the JAG prosecutor approached the bench. Tender could hear everything that was spoken, as she had very good hearing.

"Your honor, could you please ask the Colonel to either sit down or leave these proceedings?" requested Lieutenant Martone.

"The Colonel may stand or sit where he pleases. Now proceed with calling the next witness." The judge ordered. I looked at Tender in surprise, and she just lifted her shoulders and hands, palms up, as if to say she was confused too. The Colonel stood up in the back of the room with his arms crossed, and every one of the men and woman under his command stayed standing as well. I could see a new look of encouragement on the face of Captain Johansson.

"I would like to call aircraft mechanic Sergeant Daryl Roderick to the stand," said Martone, with an irritated look on his face. I was surprised to see the sergeant had a rough-looking face, was of average height, and had very dirty hands, with grease and grime under his fingernails.

"Please state your name and rank for the record," said Martone.

"DARYL RODERICK, E-6 TECHNICAL SER-GEANT," he shouted. In fact, the whole time during Lieutenant Martone's questioning, he spoke very, very, loudly!

"Sergeant Roderick, on the day in question, July 4, were you on duty?" asked Martone, raising his voice to match Daryl Roderick's tone.

"YES, SIR!" he shouted even louder. Tender was getting a kick out of the proceedings.

"On that same day, did you get one F-100 jet prepared for Captain Johansson? And you don't have to yell!" inserted Lieutenant Martone.

"YES, SIR!!" But this time he shouted even louder.

"On that day, did Captain Johansson get into the cockpit of his F-100 jet?" Martone answered, raising his voice even more. Beads of sweat were starting to form on his brow.

"YES, SIR!!" Roderick answered, now almost screaming.

"I HAVE NO MORE QUESTIONS FOR THIS WITNESS!" screamed Lieutenant Martone at the top of his voice. Tender laughed, as she was very entertained.

The judge then asked if Lieutenant Kincaid had any questions for this witness.

"Yes, your honor," replied Lieutenant Kincaid. "Sergeant Roderick, it is nice to see you again. Would you please explain your duties as an aircraft mechanic to the court?"

"I would love to; my job is to make sure the aircraft is in perfect working condition for my pilots to return to base safely, along with their aircraft. If at any time there is a problem with the aircraft, I instruct the tower commander whether it is safe to continue, or if the pilot should return to base." To our surprise, Sergeant Roderick spoke in a normal voice, clearly annoying Lieutenant Martone.

"Sergeant Roderick, do you believe in intuition?"

Lieutenant Martone jumped to his feet, "your honor, I object to this line of questioning; it is not relevant whether the Sergeant knows about intuition or not," Lieutenant Martone protested.

"Your honor, I am going to prove that the person who entered that cockpit on July 4 was, in fact, not Captain Johansson," Lieutenant Kincaid said loudly, glaring at Lieutenant Martone.

"Overruled; you may continue." The judge banged the gavel.

"Sergeant Roderick, how many years have you been keeping 'our boys' flying safely?"

"It will be twenty years in December of this year,"

"Would you say you know the habits of your pilots, like any rituals they may have?"

"Yes, I do; just like anyone who has kids knows they are all different," affirmed the sergeant.

"What are some differences of the rituals a pilot might have?"

"One of them kisses his plane before he enters the cockpit; one always does the sign of the cross in front of his plane; one kisses a picture of his wife and kids once he is in the cockpit. Things like that."

"I get the picture—they all do something that makes them unique from one another. Now suppose you never saw their face clearly; could you tell who they were by the rituals they perform or by your own intuition?"

"Without a doubt,"

"Very good. And does Captain Johansson have any such rituals he performs?"

"Yes, he always carries his helmet in his right hand, and he never puts on his leather head covering until he enters the cockpit,"

"Is there any conversation with the captain before he enters the cockpit and puts his leather head covering on, and does he always fly the same plane?"

"Yes, they tell me any problems or concerns with their plane. They name them, they paint them, they make them their own."

Lieutenant Martone jumped up. "I object, your honor. What does this have to do with the case? So, planes need tweaking at times; I feel we are wasting time with this line of questioning." His face was almost purple with frustration.

"Your honor, I am almost done with this witness, if you would just indulge me for a few more minutes."

"Overruled, you may proceed." The Judge ordered.

Just then, Tender tapped the table three times and handed Lieutenant Kincaid a note. She nodded her head in agreement.

"Sergeant, do all the pilots always ask you, before they enter the cockpit, if the repair on the report they requested, has been fixed?"

"I hardly ever have a pilot who does not speak to me before he jumps into the cockpit."

"Sergeant, please tell me: on July 4, did Captain

Johansson carry his helmet and leather cap in his right hand, swinging it as he approached?"

"No, he did not nor did he say 'Mary, Mary, Quite Contrary' is she ready to fly.'"

"Are you saying he named his plane 'Mary, Mary, Quite Contrary'?" questioned Kincaid with one eyebrow raised.

"Yes," blurted out Roderick. " On that day, he had his helmet under his left armpit, and he was wearing his leather cap. Then without a word, he jumped into the cockpit, started up the turbines, and was moving the aircraft even before the flaggers were ready."

"Sergeant, is that normal?"

"No. You never start your turbines until you receive the signal from the flagger," replied Roderick, vehemently shaking his head.

Just then, Tender tapped the table three times and handed the lieutenant a note. Kincaid looked back at Tender as if to say, 'OK'

Tender nodded her head encouragingly.

"Last question, Sergeant. From your experience of many years collaborating with pilots, do you still believe the testimony you gave earlier, that you saw Captain Johansson jump into the cockpit?"

"No. I do not believe it was Captain Johansson!"

"I have no more questions for this witness," Kincaid finished.

"Your honor the Air Force like to reexamine this witness?" asked Martone.

"You may proceed."

"Sergeant Roderick, is it possible that Captain Johansson knew he needed to act differently in order to trick you into believing it wasn't really him?" Martone asked gruffly.

"I guess anything is possible,"

"You also testified that pilots hardly ever do not speak to you before jumping into the cockpit. So, are you saying there have been times when pilots don't speak to you before entering the cockpit?

"Yes-but" started Roderick.

Lieutenant Martone put up his hand. "No further questions for this witness, your honor," said Martone, giving our table a smirk, as if to say we had just wasted our time.

"Your honor I would like to ask a follow-up question." Kincaid said.

"You may proceed."

"Sergeant after hearing all the testimony, do you still believe Captain Johansson never entered the cockpit on July 4?"

"I DO!" He yelled loudly, facing toward Lieutenant Martone.

"Sergeant, you may step down," said the judge.

"Your honor, we conclude our case," said Lieutenant Martone.

"At this time, we will take a break and return at 1400 hours," said the judge, rapping his gavel.

We all headed to the cafeteria for lunch and to rest. Everyone felt the trial was going as planned. Tender even anticipated how Lieutenant Martone would respond to Sergeant Roderick's testimony. Eventually, it was time for court to resume, so I had to gather up the team.

"All rise for the judge," called the court official.

"Please be seated. Lieutenant Kincaid, please call your first witness," instructed the judge.

"Would Mr. Lucas Pinto please come to the stand?" requested Lieutenant Kincaid. Mr. Pinto was sworn in and seated.

"Mr. Pinto, would you please tell this court where you work?" Kincaid began.

"I work at the Golden Calf Lounge, a drinking establishment,"

"Thank you. Now, on July 3, were you working behind the bar?"

"Yes, from 6 PM until 2 AM."

"On that night, do you remember serving Captain Johansson, and can you point him out?"

"You mean P.J.?" he asked as he pointed to Captain Johansson. "Oh, yeah, I served him."

"Before Captain Johansson entered the lounge, which is frequented mostly by military men and women, someone entered whom you had never seen before. Can you explain what you saw?"

"I saw the most beautiful woman come through the doors. She had golden blonde hair, and she must have been almost six feet tall. She had glowing skin, beautifully tanned. When she entered the room with that beautiful long white dress, everyone in there, at the time, wanted to help her onto her barstool." He looked around the courtroom and said, "I thought there was going to be a fight over her. Then I glanced over at the officers on duty that keep the troops in line."

"So, at this time, what did you do?"

"I went over and asked if I could get her a drink. She ordered a Mai Tai."

"Was she a regular, and did you ask her where she was from?"

"I had never seen her before, and she told me she was from Belgium." smiled Pinto reminiscently.

"So, she spoke French."

"No, definitely not French; I have never heard that accent before. It sounded like broken English."

Just then, to our surprise Lieutenant Kincaid spoke in a perfect Russian accent, as if giving her drink order.

"That's it! She had the same accent." exclaimed Pinto.

"I just spoke in a Russian accent Mr. Pinto. As Captain Johansson came through the double doors, did this woman show any interest in the men in your lounge that night?"

"No, not a one until P.J. entered the lounge. He went and sat in a booth with a few of his flying buddies. She immediately went over and almost sat on his lap. He really went into shock for a few moments, but after several drinks, they seemed like old friends. For every three drinks he had, she had one."

"Did they leave together? What condition was he in?"

"They left together at about 1 AM, and she had to help him walk. Boy, was he intoxicated."

"Did you see if she had a car?"

"No, but I heard a vehicle pull up and then drive off quickly."

Thank you, Mr. Pinto; no more questions." Lieutenant Kincaid sat back down.

"Lieutenant Martone, do you have any questions for this witness?" the judge asked.

"Yes, sir." Martone approached the witness stand. "Mr. Pinto, do you expect these members of the jury to believe that 'Cinderella' came into your lounge, bringing all her little animal friends, the glass slipper, and the stepsisters too?" Then he walked away from the stand, barking, "No more questions for this fairy tale witness."

Tender tapped the table three times and handed Lieutenant Kincaid a note.

"Your Honor, may I ask a follow-up question?" as she was glancing at the note.

"Yes, but make it quick," the judge answered, frowning.

Kincaid walked back over to Mr. Pinto and said, "Mr. Pinto, do you see in this courtroom any of the patrons who were at the bar that night, who witnessed this 'Cinderella' enter the lounge on the night of July 3?"

Mr. Pinto stood up and looked around. "Yes, ma'am, I see several. "Hi, boys!" He waved to the officers in the room, who looked sheepish.

"Your honor, if you think it is necessary, I can have Mr. Pinto identity every person who was a witness to this 'Cinderella' and have everyone testify. Alternatively, the court could advise the members it is satisfied that on the evening of July 3, 'Cinderella' entered the lounge, and in the early hours of July 3 and on July 4, she left with Captain Johansson," Lieutenant Kincaid said loudly.

The judge nodded at her. "I hereby declare that the court is satisfied that on the night of July 3, "Cinderella" entered the Golden Calf Lounge and stayed until approximately 1 AM on July 4, when she left the establishment, helping Captain Johansson out the door. At this time, we will adjourn until tomorrow at 9 AM," he said, banging his gavel.

We all headed out, while Lieutenant Martone shot us the dirtiest look. As Lieutenant Kincaid walked past, he stepped in front of her trying to intimidate her. She made a face, showing she was not pleased. "You think you're cute, huh? I am going to have you run out of the JAG Corps once I win this trial," he hissed.

Just then, Big John grabbed his arm, to let her pass. And he fell to his knees, wincing in pain. "If you ever try that again, I will break your arm!" Big John growled.

"Okay, okay. Let go." Martone begged.

Big John put his arm around her and walked her out.

"Big John may be gentle, but when he is upset, watch out," I commented.

Once we were back at the safe house, we discussed the strategy for tomorrow and how Lieutenant Martone would probably present his closing arguments. Although we felt that we had planted doubt in the jury members' minds, there was still a missing jet to account for.

Morning came quickly. We were all nervous

except Tender and Big John. No one had breakfast except David, Big John, and Tender. David said he would die if he didn't eat. We arrived early, and Richard started getting cold feet. He had changed his mind about his idea and was trying to convince Lieutenant Kincaid not to proceed.

"Too late, Richard. Either I am going to asked you to leave the courtroom, or this idea will be what wins this case." Lieutenant Kincaid retorted, her face set.

Richard just sat down with his hands over his face. Mary put her arm around him and gave him a hug. Lieutenant Martone entered the courtroom, rubbing his arm and glaring at Big John.

"Lieutenant Kincaid, you may call your next witness," the judge ordered.

"I call Captain Johansson to the stand."

The captain walked quickly up to the witness stand. He was over six feet tall, very muscular with black wavy hair. When he repeated the oath to be sworn in, he was loud enough for those in the next courtroom to hear.

"Captain, I want to take you back to the night of July 3. Did you enter the Golden Calf Lounge and sit with your friends until a beautiful woman Lieutenant is calling 'Cinderella' arrived?" Lieutenant Kincaid began..

"Yes, ma'am, I did."

Martone jumped up and roared, "I object! Lieutenant Kincaid is making fun of this proceeding, and I demand you order her to stop!" He pounded his table.

"What did you say?" The judge hit his gavel on his bench so hard that the bench shifted on the floor. "Overruled! You are the fool who first called her 'Cinderella,' so 'Cinderella' it is. Now shut up and sit down." The lieutenant looked around and sat down quietly, his face red.

"Captain, did 'Cinderella' approach you and make romantic advances toward both you and your friends?"

"No, ma'am; she was only interested in me."

Did she buy all the men in your booth drinks all night?"

"No, ma'am; just me."

"Do you remember leaving the lounge at 1 AM?"

"No, ma'am." He shook his head.

"What is the next think you remember, Captain?"

"On July 4, at 4 PM, I was being arrested and charged with treason," the captain said grimly.

"How did you feel when you were awake?"

"Ma'am, I was terribly sick, throwing up, with a splitting headache; I was so dizzy I had trouble walking, I have never had that problem after drinking to much."

"Captain, I am going to ask you to remove your right shoe and sock, please," Lieutenant Kincaid requested.

As the captain complied, Big John and David entered the area where the trial was taking place. Chaos broke out, as Lieutenant Martone ordered the military police officers to stop them. The judge was also upset and ordered both JAG officers back into his private chambers.

"Lieutenant Kincaid, what is going on?" the judge demanded.

"Your Honor, we discovered information about Captain Johansson that needs to be revealed when he was in his private quarters, unconscious. 'Cinderella' and her Russian spies used anesthesia to keep him unconscious for several hours, making it impossible for him to walk, much less to fly a jet."

"This is absurd," Martone snarled.

"Your honor, the bottom of the captain's foot shows evidence that he was given an IV with anesthesia from the Russians on the early morning hours of July 4," Kincaid said, ignoring Martone's glares.

The judge considered Kincaid request thoughtfully for a long moment. Finally, he said, "Although it is a strange request, court evidence can be either in paper form or live, so I will allow the bottom of the captain's foot as evidence."

All three filed back into the court room, and the judge said, "I cannot allow civilians into this area. However, I request a few military volunteers from the attendees to come forward." Every military officer in the courtroom stood to volunteer. The judge selected two large men to help. Back in the courtroom the judge ordered the captain to be brought before him to view the puncture wound between his big toe and second toe. The prosecutors and jury were all allowed to see the bottom of his foot with a magnifying glass.

"Let me explain what happened. On July 3, the captain was tempted by a beautiful woman, who then brought him home and put him in bed. A few hours after 1 PM 'Cinderella' and her Russian spies then proceeded to hang an IV bag with anesthesia in it, placing the needle between his toes to hide the puncture. This would keep the captain unconscious for the next several hours. This allowed the Russians to use a look-a-like Russian pilot to steal an F-100 fighter jet." The lieutenant walked away, lifting her hands in the air and saying, "I have nothing more."

The judge looked at Lieutenant Martone. "Does the prosecution, wish to question this witness?"

"Yes, your honor," Martone said, approaching the witness stand. "Captain, do you remember signing this confession statement, admitting to stealing one F-100 jet?"

"Yes, I do, but—"

"So, your answer is yes, correct?" Martone interrupted.

"Yes." The captain growled.

"Captain, can you explain how you received one million dollars from a Russian bank, which was deposited into a French bank account in your name on July 3?" Without waiting for an answer, Martone spun around with his right hand in the air; he was so confident that this was all he needed to condemn the captain. He then handed the bank statement as evidence to the clerk.

Tender tapped the table three times, and Lieutenant Kincaid took the note and just smiled at Tender.

"No more questions for 'Benedict Arnold,' said Martone scathingly. Then he strolled back to his seat.

"Your honor, I would like to ask a follow-up question, please," Lieutenant Kincaid requested.

"You may proceed."

"Captain, on what day did you sign that confession statement, and were you advised to have a JAG officer represent you before signing any statements?" Kincaid asked the captain.

"I was terribly sick, so I think it was the same day, July 4. I was never offered any legal representation," the captain replied. A murmur broke out in the courtroom.

The judge banged the gavel to bring court to order. "Jury members, that confession statement is not admissible, as it was obtained without a JAG officer being assigned to the captain to review any statements he would be signing. Therefore, you members of the jury are not to consider that as a confession of guilt; rather, you may only consider what evidence you acquire at these hearings."

I looked over at Lieutenant Martone; he was clenching his teeth in anger.

"We will take a two-hour break for lunch and meet back here at 2 PM for closing arguments," said the judge, dismissing the court. Everyone stood as the judge left.

Once in the cafeteria, Lieutenant Kincaid wanted to go over Tender's approach to the final arguments, but Tender refused and asked to be left alone the entire time.

"Elaine, isn't she going to take some notes or something? She looks like she is sleeping. Is she all, right? I need to go and help her," the lieutenant said, started to stand up.

Big John grabbed her by the shoulders. "Lieutenant, you are watching the most amazing little genius work her magic. Just sit tight, relax, and take a deep breath." The lieutenant reluctantly followed his advice.

Time seemed to drag on, as every eye was on Tender. At the end of the two hours, she suddenly popped up, walked over, and just said, "Let's go."

David looked at me. "She is ready," I said.

As we entered the courtroom, we noticed Lieutenant Martone and his staff were all standing and watching us enter, and they didn't look happy. Tender just smiled at them as she walked by.

"Lieutenant Martone are you ready with your closing statement?" began the judge, looking over at Martone.

"Yes, your honor," replied Martone. He walked over and stood in front of the members of the jury.

"Gentleman, why are we here? This is not just a horse-and-pony show. We are here because I proved that on July 4, Captain Johansson boarded the cockpit of 'Mary, Mary, Quite Contrary'. He then flew it to Russia and received one million dollars for a plane that cost thirty-five million American dollars. We know the jet mechanic witnessed the captain entering the cockpit on July 4. We now believe he had a Russian girlfriend with whom he was in love, and both were in on the plan. I believe he planned to skip out before we noticed the plane was missing, but because he had a hangover from the night before, he slept a

little too late. Even the puncture on the bottom of his foot was planned so that if he was caught, he could say the Russians drugged him and took his plane. Nice try, Captain. I believe the defense has proved nothing except concocting what might make a good children's story: 'The little captain who could.' I am asking you members of the jury to convict Captain Peter Johansson during this court-martial of treason against the United States of America, and to make sure Captain Johansson is put to death. Thank you." Martone was smiling from ear to ear as he returned to his seat.

"Defense, are you ready to give your closing statement?" the judge asked. A long, three-foot-wide by twelve-foot-long walking box was constructed for Tender so she could be eye to eye with the members of the jury. Lieutenant Kincaid and Tender approached the jury. Lieutenant Kincaid allowed Tender to address them. Her neck was wet from sweat. I began to worry that the Lieutenant was having a panic attack.

Tender first thanked every member of the jury by name and rank, saluting each one as she stood in front of them. Every one of them never stopped smiling. This was bothering Lieutenant Martone.

"Gentlemen, first, I want to thank you for your service. My grandpa fought in the U.S. military, and I sure love him. Sorry, but he was in the United States Navy." The jury members. all laughed. I noticed Lieutenant Kincaid relaxing also laughed, as she stayed close to Tender.

"This is one case I do believe the prosecution should have dismissed once he saw all the evidence. I know you are thinking the same, but to make sure you understand what actually happened on July 3, and 4, I will present enough evidence so Captain Johansson will be back in the cockpit by tomorrow." As she turned, she pointed his way.

"On July 3, which was not his day to report to duty. Captain Johansson was instructed on some difficult maneuvers in which he would be testing the F-100 on the morning of July 4. Captain Johansson is a test pilot, not a fighter pilot; his job is to take 'Mary, Mary Quite Contrary' on interesting maneuvers. Captain Johansson is the top pilot in the Air Force, but was not in 1954 when this jet made its debut. His F-100 Super Sabre supersonic jet was designed by North American Aviation."

"This beautiful plane weighs in at 21,000 pounds, is faster than a speeding bullet at 864 miles per hour. This plane can fly as high as 50,000 feet and can travel 1,995 miles on a full tank of fuel. How do we know all these statistics are correct? Because," Tender turned around and pointed to

Captain Johansson, "that Air Force hero was willing to make sure they were. So yes, he filled up the tank and flew till he would be out of fuel just as he landed. Now that's scary. He once flew to 50,610 feet before descending, but when he reached that height, the plane was shaking so badly he thought it was going to break into pieces. That is why he put the maximum height at 50,000 feet. Once he pushed 'Mary, Mary Quite Contrary' to 1,001 miles per hour and one of his turbines shut down, but he was able to restart the turbine and land safely. I personally think he is nuts. If I were you and you were going on a trip with this captain, I would say don't let him drive. He just might try to break the land speed record." The place exploded with laughter, and even the judge was laughing. I noticed Lieutenant Kincaid clapping and laughing.

"Now that we have established what Captain Johansson is willing to do for his country, let us look at the evidence. On July 3, Captain Johansson was misled by a beautiful woman. You heard the bartender testify that he heard a vehicle approach and then leave in a hurry. The captain was so intoxicated it was easy for 'Cinderella' and her Russian spies to lead the captain up to his room. I believe he was still semiconscious, so they used a little ether to make sure he was out cold. You saw the black-and-blue bruises and the small needle hole in the bottom of his foot. If they had used his arm, it would take days for the bruise to heal, and everyone would know he was drugged." Tender stopped and closed her eyes with both hands on her face as she used her recall.

"The captain was given an IV with anesthesia. The side effects are dizziness, bruising, nausea and vomiting, shivering and feeling cold, sore throat, and confusion. Some of these side effects are experienced when a person is intoxicated. Another interesting fact is that while under anesthesia you are very suggestible. So, if you hear the sounds of a jet turbine engine and voices from the tower giving you instructions, you will believe that these things are really happening around you and that you are the pilot of your plane. As I have said, the captain was in a semi-comatose state, not quite totally in a deep sleep, but he would not be able to wake up. That explains why Captain Johansson believed he was in the plane; his neighbors have said they heard the sound of a jet plane coming from his room, but they thought nothing of it. They thought he was listening to a training tape. Now, because he lives off base we will not hear from his civilian neighbors. The prosecution was given notice to question any of the captain's neighbors, and could have brought contrary evidence, but came forward with none.

Adding up all the evidence this proves he was being set up. Remember when I told you this aircraft can fly 1,995 miles on a full tank, but that would require 630 gallons of fuel? But on July 4, it only had about 350 gallons, for a flight distance of about 1100 miles. The prosecutor claims that we are telling a fairy tale; well, he should check his facts, because he is uninformed for such a smart officer. The distance from the base in Maryland to the closest airstrip in Russia is 5,830 miles. Now, Lieutenant Martone claimed the captain flew a total of 5,830 miles on half a tank of fuel. If the captain had tried to fly all the way to Russia, he would have crashed in Canada, but here he sits. I believe the F-100 jet plane is still in the United States in a small hangar, just waiting for the best military in the world to bring 'Mary, Mary Quite Contrary' home."

The judge stood up abruptly. "Tender Purdy, what makes you think our F-100 is still in the United States?" he said sharply.

"Simple—with every crime, mistakes are made. All piston-powered airplanes such as smaller planes run on 100LL aviation fuel. This jet plane only runs on JP-4 or JP-5 turbine fuel. The government controls this fuel, so the plane is still here awaiting refueling. So, what we have is a F-100 sitting in a hangar and waiting for a tanker with JP-4 or JP-5 fuel.

Every single person in that room, including

the members of the jury, stood up and cheered. Big John lifted Tender in the air. Lieutenant Linda Kincaid ran over to Tender and gave her a kiss on the cheek. "You are amazing! I love you, Tender." Tender just smiled.

Suddenly, the judge hit his gavel so hard that he broke the handle. "Would everyone please be seated!" he ordered loudly. As the room quieted down, the judge looked around the room sternly. "We still have a trial to complete. Tender, are you finished with your closing statements?"

"Yes, your honor," she replied.

"Very well; let's adjourn until tomorrow, and we will resume when the jury members have reached a verdict," said the judge.

"Your honor, the jury requests to hand down their verdict at this time." said the head juror, standing and addressing the judge.

"Very well; regarding the accusation of the theft of the supersonic jet committed by Captain Peter Johansson, how do you find?" asked the judge.

All eight members came back with a verdict of not guilty.

"Regarding the charge of treason against the United States and receiving the death penalty, how do you find Captain Peter Johansson?"

All eight members saluted Captain Peter

Johansson and repeated one at a time, "Not guilty." The judge then concluded the proceedings and dismissed the court.

Captain Johansson's parents immediately ran to hug their son, weeping uncontrollably. Lieutenant Martone came over and shook Tender's hand, saying, "You did good, kid. I think I learned something this week."

"And what is that?" asked Lieutenant Kincaid.

"Never mess with girl power!" he said, shaking his head.

We all laughed, and Lieutenant Martone invited us all to a fancy dinner, on him. During the dinner, we realized that Lieutenant Martone and his staff were actually very nice, and they took their obligation to uphold the law very seriously. Everyone was surprised when Tender wanted to make a toast. As she lifted her glass of lemonade, she said, "I would like to toast the two lieutenants, and I hope they invite us all to the wedding."

Everyone cried out, "No way." The two Lieutenants just smiled at each other.

"Tender, how did you know?" asked Lieutenant Kincaid in disbelief.

"I noticed how you would look at him every time we were in the court room, and every time we left you exchanged notes. I figured you are allowed to date each other except when you enter the courtroom. I also figured out you weren't being held back because you are a woman; it was because you were dating the second-best JAG officer in your unit," Tender smiled.

"Wait a minute, you mean the best JAG officer in our unit." Martone corrected with a smile.

"Not anymore. There's a new sheriff in town," boomed Big John Riley. Everyone clapped for Lieutenant Kincaid. Lieutenant Martone gave her a big kiss and said, "I don't mind being number two to you!"

"You better get used to it," said David teasingly.

I gently punched him in the arm. "What does that mean, David?"

"Nothing, dear." he said innocently.

Everyone was exhausted; it had been a long week, and we all agreed that we wanted to fly home the next morning. But just then, Director Lance, who was still in shock that we were able to help Captain Johansson gave us an interesting note to read. He handed it to me, and I read it aloud.

"Hello, Team Purdy, this is your President. I just heard the good news from Secretary Johansson, Captain Johansson's father. The country is proud of every one of you. I have directed the FBI and the CIA to find my stolen plane. Before you leave tomorrow, you will have lunch with me at the White House. Be here at noon and dress casual. This is an order, but I promise I will get you home before dark."

Tender started jumping up and down with joy. However, when we returned to the safe house Vicky was confused as to why the President would bother to call us. I explained that this was an enormous case, and he was relieved his Secretary of the Navy did not have to resign his post.

TWELVE

Tender Visits the White House

We all had to wake-up early, as we would need time to freshen up before our one-hour drive to the White House. Once we arrived, we were escorted to the south gate, where we were greeted by some Secret Service agents. Everyone who had a weapon had to surrender it, and all the weapons were placed in a locked vault with a tag with the owners name on it. Only Director Lance was allowed to keep his weapon. For the next hour, we were given a private tour by the First Lady, and she and Tender became fast friends. She was so funny. It is amazing how normal famous people are in real life. She had grown up on a farm, milking cows and shoveling manure, and she was teasing Tender by saying how much she missed the smell.

Afterward, we were invited into the President's

private residence. Over lunch, I was surprised that the President was such a wonderful listener. He wanted to know everything in detail about how we put the pieces together; he seemed fascinated by every word we spoke. As we were leaving, he informed us that the plane was recovered in the state of Iowa, and several Russian spies had been captured, including 'Cinderella.' He got a kick out of the name we used to describe the woman who seduced Captain Johansson. We left the White House with an experience we would never forget. On our way out, the President said something amazing.

"When I was a boy, I wanted to be a man, but now that I am a man, I wish I were a boy and that Tender Purdy was my best friend. Tender, are you my friend?" he asked with a smile.

"You bet I am." she replied as they hugged. I just put my hands over my mouth.

"Even the President of the United States wants to be Tender's friend." Well, of course he does," said Big John with a chuckle.

Meanwhile, David was complaining he was starving. I sympathized; the portions at lunch had been small, even for me.

After an uneventful flight, we arrived home just as it was getting dark. We picked up pizza on the way home and counted all our blessings. Since the next day was Sunday, I contacted everyone and let them know we were back and would be picking up Mrs. Hines and Skippy in the morning. Sunday dinner was quiet at Alex and Loriann's taco buffet; we were all exhausted. Even Tender just rested all day with Skippy on her lap.

Everyone wanted to know what case we were working on. David told some vague highlights of our adventure without revealing anything about this top-secret case. He did talk about our visit to the White House, meeting the President and First Lady and, of course, about all the good food he had eaten. To us it was remembered as 'just another day in the office.' We looked at each other knowing that this was one case that would never be recorded in our registry of solved cases. Tender went on to tell how wonderfully the President and First Lady had treated us.

THIRTEEN

Tender and the Amusement Park

Monday morning came, and we all headed to FBI headquarters. We had finished our military case just in time for our upcoming vacation, in a week. First, we headed to the cafeteria for breakfast, and then we made our way to Director Lance's office for a quick briefing. Director Lance gave us our instructions to report back next Monday packed and ready to go. We spent the week reviewing some cold cases and decided a few were either accidents or so old we would not be able to close them. Tender agreed on all the cases, so the week went by quickly and we were able to close four unsolved cases, which made Chief Purdy happy, as his quarterly report was due. He knew the cold case unit was still under the microscope.

Sunday came and Tender and Anne were so

excited they didn't seem to pay attention in church. During dinner at Grandma and Grandpa's house all they could talk about was the park and what they wanted to see. Big John was driving Alex crazy over the addition on the house. I never saw Alex and Loriann so happy to leave as they kissed Anne goodbye. I was even getting a headache. Once home and in bed I had to go into the girls' room to quiet them down.

Monday morning came and David was not happy that breakfast was going to be served on the plane, he was sure it would not be enough for him. Finally, we all made our way to the airfield to board a private jet. Our group included David and me, Big John, Vicky, Tender, and Anne, and of cause, Richard and Mary. To our surprise, Agent Dwayne Sisson was on board, and he introduced us to his wife, Eileen, and their son, Derek.

"Good morning, Purdys. I received the same gift as you at the awards ceremony. I hope you are okay with us coming along for the ride?" asked Agent Sisson

I replied warmly, "We are excited, not only to have you with us but also to meet your family."

Tender asked Derek to sit with her, Vicky, and Anne and introduced everyone right away.

Derek was excited to meet Tender. "I have had

heard that you are the smartest five-year-old in the country." Derek said admiringly.

"I doubt that. I just see things differently than other children my age," Tender laughed.

Anne looked anxiously around the plane and asked, "Tender, is this plane safe?"

"Absolutely!" Tender replied enthusiastically. "It is a Grumman Gulfstream, weighing 65,500 pounds. It has two Rolls-Royce Dart turboprop engines, which are good for long-range trips. It can hold up to fifteen passengers."

Derek replied, "That is fantastic. I can't wait to see this plane in action." The children all sat together, with two of the seats facing the other, and the adults did the same in the aisle across from them. Since Derek was closer to Vicky's age, he sat next to her. Tender and Anne sat next to each other.

Then the pilot began the announcements. "Good morning everyone; my name is Agent Gregory. Please buckle your seat belts. We will be taking off in a few minutes to California. The flight time is three hours and twenty-two minutes. The weather for flying is clear. The temperature in Anaheim today is eighty-six degrees, with sunny skies."

Agent Carrie Jackson, the flight attendant, came out of the cockpit and greeted everyone.

"Hello, everyone. It's nice to see you all again

so soon. For those of you who don't know me, my name is Agent Jackson, but you can call me C.J. Good morning, Agent Sisson, and Team Purdy. There are a few faces here I don't recognize. I would like to guess the names of the passengers I don't know. Let me see; are you Mrs. Eileen Sisson?" She went on and guessed everyone by name.

"Yes. You did perfectly," Tender said with a smile.

"And of course, I know Agent John Riley," Carrie said, beaming at Big John.

"C.J., so nice to see you again," Big John said, standing up and sweeping her into a Big John hug.

After Big John had let go, Carrie straightened up and said to Tender, "Say, Tender, I've heard you can tell a lot about a person just by looking at them. What can you tell about me?"

I jumped in and said, "Be careful. You might not want to go there."

"Yes, I do. Let's see what you have, Tender."

Tender looked her over, and even checked her hands. Finally, she said, "Well, you are from a cold climate, most likely close to Boston. You were engaged, but you recently broke it off. You are now involved with Agent Gregory. You have not been an agent for more than a few years. You love seafood."

"Okay, I am sorry I asked. Everything you said is correct. How did you know all that?" Carrie exclaimed.

"Well, I knew you were from a cold climate because your hands are all cracked, and I can smell the lotion you need to soften them. You are from near Boston because you do not pronounce your *R*'s. I can tell you were engaged, because you still have the mark where the diamond ring was on your finger. And I know you are involved with Agent Gregory because I noticed your red lipstick is smudged from kissing before we boarded the plane, and I also saw him give you a quick wink while we were walking toward the plane. And finally, I can smell seafood on your clothing." Tender smiled.

"Well, you are amazing. And I want to let you all know that Agent Gregory and I have permission from headquarters to be seeing each other," Carrie. said, blushing.

"I guessed that, or I wouldn't have mentioned it. All agents who are involved with another agent in a relationship must disclose their relationships to their department heads," Tender nodded.

The time went by fast, as the kids played games and guessed what kind of clouds they were passing. Tender was excited to learn that Vicky knew every type of cloud formation. Tender had never been very interested in astronomy or meteorology.

Finally, we landed at Anaheim airport. FBI Agent Carlos Ramos was there with a limousine to escort us to the FBI log cabin. It was about a thirty-five-minute drive out in the woods.

Once we arrived, we could see that the cabin was breathtaking. It overlooked a beautiful lake, and was surrounded by daffodils, daisies, chrysanthemums, and different colors of roses. I gasped in delight.

When we entered the cabin, it was like no cabin any of us had ever seen. The whole cabin was built of redwood, with beautiful winding redwood stairs. It had seven bedrooms and seven bathrooms. The two boys, Richard, and Derek, were in a room with two twin beds. Tender, Anne, Vicky, and Mary were in one large room together, with two sets of bunk beds. Agent Sisson and Eileen were in a room with a king-size bed. David and I were in the largest suite, which had an extra-long king-size bed, a large bathroom with a heart-shaped whirlpool tub, and a large shower. Finally, Big John had the smallest room with a queen-size bed. There was also a beautifully furnished sitting room. The cabin had a fully functioning kitchen, which was also constructed from redwood, and the smell of the wood was wonderful.

As Agent Sisson walked us around the cabin, he told us that he had been there before with other supervisors from across the country. He also informed us that it was called the Garden Retreat.

The night before, we had decided to eat all our meals out so we would not have to cook. The park was open from 8 AM to 11 PM. for FBI agents and guests. We were also given FBI wristbands, which allowed us to skip the lines.

Tender, Anne, Vicky, and their new friend Derek were up at dawn, ready for an exciting adventure. I woke up soon after the kids. "Good morning, children. The adults will be ready soon, and then we will leave," I reported.

"Mom, Vicky and I already memorized the park map from the brochure we received in the mail," Tender told me excitedly.

"Okay. We will follow you children wherever you lead us, but breakfast first," David said with a yawn, shuffling out of the bathroom.

Everyone got ready at about the same time. "Okay, let's hit the road." exclaimed our driver for the week, Agent Ramos. It took about forty minutes to get to the park, since we hit traffic. Then Agent Ramos dropped us off at the front gate.

"I will go and park the limo and catch up with you. Where should I meet you?" Agent Ramos asked.

Tender instructed him to take the monorail to Apple Pie Station. We were going to the Apple Pie Diner for breakfast.

"Thank you, Tender. See you soon." he said.

As we entered the first area of the park, Country Road U.S.A, every building looked like it came from a storybook. Tender pointed to a castle and said, "That is where my prince lives." We all laughed and agreed with her assessment.

When we boarded the train, we could all see the excitement in the eyes of the children. I was especially glad to see Tender act her age. The train sounded its horn, and then we were off to the next stop, Apple Square. The monorail was such a fun ride. I asked David to sit with me in the rear of the train so we could talk in private. Big John always sat near Tender and Vicky. Vicky never let go of Tender's hand.

"David, I have a suspicion that Agents Sisson and Ramos are here on official business," I said quietly in his ear.

"Elaine, why do you think that?" he said, putting his arm around me to make it look like we were cuddling.

"Who comes to the amusement park wearing a suit, unless they are carrying a weapon and are on duty?" I pointed out.

"So, what would be their motive for not telling us?" David muttered; his brows furrowed.

"David, I believe they are both here to protect Tender and keep her safe." I said, nodding at Tender.

"I see; they are concerned she is a valuable asset and always in danger," David said thoughtfully. "Well, Elaine, I will approach both the agents and question them." I smiled at him and gave him a quick kiss.

It was a beautiful sunny day, and we finally arrived at Apple Square. The architecture of all the buildings in this part of the park reminded us of France.

"Tender, what kind of buildings are we looking at?" I asked.

"Mom, that building is a Creole cottage with a balcony. Although several of the buildings are Egyptian Revival, they all have balconies. That building on the corner is a French revival church. I also noticed an exceedingly rare Baroque Cabildo. Some are Greek revival styles. All these buildings are from the late 1700's."

"Thank you for the history lesson," I smiled. It is nice having a walking, talking encyclopedia on hand.

"Tender is there anything you don't know about?" asked Derek.

"Derek, I still have so much to learn. I also know

that only with God's help will I ever find wisdom, which I lack."

Finally, Tender pointed to a long building with an awning. "Here we are at the Apple Diner." Everyone was hungry for breakfast. Just then, Agent Ramos appeared and joined us.

"Agent Sisson and Agent Ramos, can I speak to you both for a minute?" David asked, nodding at them.

"Certainly," they both replied. They followed David into a side corner, and I joined them.

"Elaine and I are wondering why you are both dressed in suits and ties at an amusement park?" David said pointedly.

Special Agent Sisson spoke. "We have been assigned to protect Tender, as she is the most valuable asset the FBI has. We are also allowed to inform you that we have a janitor at the Montessori school to protect her."

"How about at our home?" I asked.

"No. We understand you would give your life for her. So would Agent Riley, Agent Ramos, and I," Agent Sisson replied.

"Why do you think that she needs protection here?" I asked worriedly.

"It has been our experience that anyone who helps the FBI could be a target, and Director Lance is not going to allow that to happen to Agent Tender." Agent Sisson said vehemently.

David and I thanked them for their explanation. David was satisfied, but I was still concerned that this would affect our family vacation.

Breakfast was served buffet-style, so it didn't take long for everyone to pile up their plates and fill up with food.

As the day went on, the children enjoyed themselves, going on rides and exploring the park. We spent most of the day in Country Road U.S.A. Finally, at the end of the day, Agent Ramos drove us back.

Once we were back at the Garden Retreat, even though we were tired, Big John, David, and I took a walk to the lake. When we got down to the beach, I turned and looked at Big John.

"So, Big John what is going on?" I asked. I explained our conversation with Agent Sisson to him.

Big John nodded. "I am not surprised, because Tender told me she had seen one of the janitors from her school at FBI headquarters recently. I thought she was mistaken."

"Elaine, I am okay with it, as long as you are?" David shot a questioning look at me.

I did not answer right away. Instead, I picked up

a stone from the beach and looked at it for a while. "Well, I am relieved to know she is being always protected, especially since I do not think we can stop what she loves to do. She loves to help those in need, even though so many of these cases are extremely dangerous." I replied finally.

We made our way back up to the house. Tender came up to us and said, "So, are we all set?"

"What do you mean, Tender?" I asked, puzzled.

"Are you okay with Agent Sisson and Agent Ramos being here to protect me?" she said, with her arms crossed.

"Tender, darling, how did you know that?" I asked.

"I knew that I was protected at school; I am protected even when I go out to play. The FBI agent posing as a janitor always comes out holding a broom and sits on a bench and watches me. And anytime agents wear a suit, it means they are on duty and are carrying a gun. Also, at the park today, I noticed several agents watching me," Tender explained.

"Tender, we can stop all this. You can stop solving cases if you are afraid," David said, bending down and putting his arm around Tender.

"No, Dad and Mom. God has given me a special gift, and I love helping people," Tender replied, shaking her head vehemently.

"Okay. Then we are all in agreement; right, Elaine?" David said.

I replied, "Yes, I guess we are." I bent down and hugged Tender and David.

David and I spoke to Agent Sisson and let him know we were all right with the protection detail that was watching Tender. He then surprised us and gave me a gun to put in my purse. I signed a carry permit issued from the FBI in my name.

The week was going splendidly, and the weather stayed beautiful; we only had light showers on the fifth day, and we had seen all the park could offer. We visited Frog Land, Apple Land, and Tornado Land, and we saw fireworks every night. The food was excellent, except for the weight we probably all were putting on. The kids loved being followed by park characters. We knew the FBI had arranged this, when all day long we met every princess and prince who walked with us entertaining the kids.

It was on the sixth day that something unexpected happened. There was a knock on the door, and Agents Sisson and Ramos drew their guns and approached the door with caution. Tender and all the children went upstairs to a safe room.

"This is Agent Sisson; who is it? Please identify yourself!" Agent Sisson barked.

"Special Agent Allen Connor," came the reply.

Agent Sisson knew him, and he opened the door. They shook hands, and then Agent Connor waved his hand, and ten more agents entered the cabin.

"What can I do for you, Allen?" asked Agent Sisson, holstering his gun.

"We need help with a case, Agent Sisson. We were informed Agent Tender Purdy was coming to town, and we have been doing surveillance everywhere she goes," Agent Connor responded.

Agent Sisson went upstairs and asked Tender, David, Big John, and me to come downstairs.

Richard blurted out, "Wait a minute. Mary and I are part of Team Purdy; why are we not invited?"

"Sorry; please join us," Agent Sisson acknowledged, motioning for him and Mary to come along.

Once downstairs, Tender asked, "Agent Sisson, what is going on? Do we have a case?"

"Yes, it looks like it, Tender."

Tender looked around the room and said, "Mom and Dad, I would like to introduce you to all the agents watching us at the park this week."

I spoke up. "Please don't ask how she knows that; she just does."

"Tender, and Mrs. and Mr. Purdy, it is so nice to meet you. My name is Special Agent Allen Connor," as he started shaking hands. Then we introduced him to Richard and Mary. It turned out he already knew Big John.

"Nice to meet you, Agent Connor," we all said.

David asked, "What is this case about?"

One of the agents set up a chalkboard in the meeting room that had been locked. It was a large room, with a long table, surrounded by fifteen chairs. The agent opened a large closet and pulled out a large easel corkboard and started tacking up pictures.

Once the board was full of crime scene pictures, Special Agent Connor laid out his case.

"Twenty-two days ago, at the amusement park, in Apple Pie Trail, before the park opened, one of the park workers from the cleaning crew found a young woman lying unconscious on a park bench." He pointed to the picture. She had a head wound, as he also pointed out on the picture. "No one has reported her as a missing person," he continued.

Tender asked, "Has she come out of her coma?"

"Yes, she has, but she has amnesia," replied Agent Connor.

Team Purdy went right into action. We all came up to the board and started to study the pictures up close.

"Look at the size of that wound," David noted.

"Please get us the measurements of the size of the wound," I asked. As Agent Connor was about to tell us the size of the wound, Tender held up her hand and stopped him.

I spoke up. "Actually, Agent Connor, Tender will tell you the size of the wound." I nodded at Tender.

She asked, "Did you measure in centimeters or inches?"

"Centimeters," replied Agent Connor, looking at Tender curiously.

"Very well; the wound is 12.70 centimeters by 2.8 centimeters."

Agent Connor jumped back and exclaimed, "No way. How could you know that so precisely?"

"Easy; she was struck by a golf club, most likely a number one-wood with a 60-degree angle, as the wound is deeper at the top. She was struck by the heel first, then the toe. This would indicate the attacker was shorter by a few inches. I noticed she is five foot nine, so the attacker is five foot three or so."

"Anything else you can tell us?" Agent Connor said in wonder.

"The attacker is left-handed and very strong, based on the depth of the wound," Tender continued.

"So, it is most likely a man?" Agent Connor pressed.

"No. It is most likely a young woman, who is a particularly good golfer, almost a professional."

Tender stood up. "We need to visit the victim in the hospital,"

On our way to the secure ward in the hospital, Richard asked Agent Sisson "why it had been so quiet in the room."

Big John interrupted and answered, "There is not an agent in the FBI who doesn't want to be in the same room as Tender and watch her do her magic. And that includes Agent Ramos and Agent Connor."

Agent Ramos, who was driving the limo, shouted from the front, "Amen to that."

Tender tugged at my sleeve. "Mom, I feel so bad for this young woman."

"I know, darling, so do I." I said, putting my arm around her.

"I believe she might have a lot in common with you mom, I mean that she was an orphan, and she graduated from college without anyone looking out for her. That might be why no one came to identify her." Tender guessed.

"Then, we must help her find her way back home." I said, giving her a squeeze.

As we reached the hospital, Tender asked Agent Connor to bring a set of golf clubs. It just happened that one of the agents had a set.

As Team Purdy entered the room, we saw the young women lying on a hospital bed. She was so pretty. She had blue eyes and naturally blonde hair.

What kind of evil person would harm this young lady?

When she saw the golf clubs, she called out, "Are those mine?"

"Good morning, my name is Tender Purdy."

Just then, one of the agents brought over a step stool so Tender could be face-to-face with 'Jane Doe.'

She replied, "Good morning, do I know you?"

"No, you don't, but I am going to help you understand what happened to you."

'Jane Doe' shook her head. "You are only a child; how are you going to help me?"

Tender replied, "I am an FBI agent who helps in difficult cases." She smiled reassuringly at her.

"Okay, Tender, please help me. I am so afraid, and no one seems to want me." she said with a sob.

"Can I see your hands?" asked Tender.

'Jane Doe' looked surprised, but she held out her hands for Tender to see. Tender examined them and said, "The attacker used a chemical to remove her fingerprints, because all college athletes are fingerprinted." As Tender continued studying her hands, she said, "You are a right-handed golfer, and an incredibly good one. I would guess to get calluses like these, you practice hours each day."

"Is that why I recognized golf clubs?" 'Jane Doe' asked eagerly.

"Yes. Golf is your whole life. I am going to feed you facts, and I want you to see if you can identify the golf course I am describing."

'Jane Doe' nodded, and Tender went on. "This course was built in 1927. Peter Coin and Michael Baker designed it. It overlooks a river. It is a par seventy and has 7,225 yards of fairways. It is regarded as one of the most beautiful courses in the world, and the most beautiful in America. Surprisingly, it is a public course, not private."

She yelled out, "Cable River, in Cable, California!"

"Agent Connor, please contact Cable River and inquire if there was a WPGA qualifying tournament there about twenty-two days ago," requested Tender.

Agent Connor pointed to one of the agents, and he got right on it.

"Okay, I am going to give you some other facts," Tender continued.

"You are right-handed; you might be an orphan, just like my mom. My guess is you graduated college within the last few years. If you played golf in college, you might be ranked. If you were ranked, you should have been invited on the amateur golf tour which travels around the world with the top twenty four best amateur golfers. If you were ranked among the top 10 in the world you would be invited to qualifying in the WGPA. The WPGA was founded in 1950 at Rolling Hills Country Club in Wichita, Kansas" Tender said briskly. "Someone needed to get rid of you because you were one of the top five in the tournament. Since you were most likely practicing late, that was the ideal time to get rid of you. The opportunity arose, and you were attacked."

"But how did I get here?" 'Jane Doe' asked in amazement.

"The attacker drove you 350 miles, and then she drove back and typed a note saying you could not take the pressure and were withdrawing from the tournament. They couldn't sign your name on the note, since they are left-handed, and you are right-handed. Lefties slant their letters to the left when they write." Tender said.

Just then, Agent Connor received the information from Cable River and handed it to Big John.

"There was a WPGA amateur qualifying tournament around the time she was found," reported Big John.

"I also informed headquarters to investigate who left the tournament early. We should know in a few days," he nodded at 'Jane Doe.'

'Jane Doe' looked at Tender and started crying. "I will never forget you, Tender Purdy. Thank you so much."

Every agent started clapping and cheering, "Tender. Tender. Tender."

Agent Connor patted Tender on the back. "Tender, I have never seen anything like this in my fifteen years as an agent. You sure are special!"

We were all tired and ready to go home to North Dakota. When we landed at the airport, a limousine was waiting to take us home. Over the next few weeks, Tender was given some time off. Meanwhile, David and I went to work picking out the top three candidates from those who signed up to be on our cold case team.

Finally, we were asked to report to FBI headquarters, and were escorted to Director Lance's office.

"Good day, Purdys. The park has sent you a reward for solving the 'Theme Park Bench' case. One of the competitors, Justine Grant, was in sixth place, with no way to qualify for one of the top five spots, which she needed in order to end up on the WPGA tour. Diane Shelby was in the top spot, and she was the only golfer who had no relative waiting for her. Therefore, she was the only one Justine could dispose of without raising suspicion," Director Lance said. "The good news is that Diane Shelby has fully recovered and is now on the tour. She will be in North Dakota next month, and she wants to spend time with Tender," said Director Lance.

FOURTEEN

Paula Hand Comes on Board

The director looked down and shuffled some papers on his desk before looking up again. He gave us a wry smile. "I am sure the last thing you want right now is another case," he said.

David looked at me. "The team loves FBI cases," I said, with a thumbs-up from David.

"Yes, I am sure the team will be all in" he said.

Director Lance brought us into the investigation room, and it was loaded with pictures and evidence. We looked around, but we quickly realized we needed the whole team there. "Director Lance, we will return after the weekend with the whole team," David reported.

"Thank you, Purdys; see you on Monday," Director Lance said, as he saw us out.

Once back at police headquarters, we cleared

our upcoming FBI time with Chief Purdy and got his permission to help the FBI on another case.

Friday night was pizza night with a meeting. When we picked up Tender and Vicky from school and drove home, we saw that Richard and Mary were already there waiting for us. "Richard, I love your 1961 Impala convertible," Vicky signed.

Mary injected, "You mean *our* 1961 Impala." Everyone laughed.

After pizza, David called a meeting.

"We have a new case with the FBI. We will meet with Director Lance on Monday to find out the details." Everyone nodded.

"Next, we need to choose one new detective to add to our team for all our cold cases," David continued.

Richard raised his hand. "Does that mean Mary and I are not going to be part of the team?"

"On the contrary; you both will be consultants, like Tender, to the Bismarck police department. However, the position does not come with pay," replied David.

I described the list of candidates. "David and I have narrowed it down to three candidates at police headquarters. The first is Detective Jane Woodward. She has been on the force six years, and has been a detective for two of those years. She was just married last year. She and her partner, Frank Stone, have solved the most cases, at twenty-seven out of thirty. Only David and I, along with Team Purdy, have solved one hundred percent of our cases, but we didn't solve twenty-seven. She is known to be incredibly quiet, until she knows the answer.

"Candidate number two is Andrew Capozzoli. He has been on the force twenty-two years and has been a detective for fifteen years. He is one of the best detectives we have, and he is always given difficult cases. He is forty-two years old, smart and always to the point, married with five children.

Candidate number three is Paula Hand. She has been on the force four years, like David and I. She also made detective after her third year. She is twenty-five years old, not married, and she finished top out of the women in the state police training. Like me, she finished top in hand-to-hand combat."

David said, "Now we need to choose one of these three. First, we will narrow it down by eliminating one, so please write down on your pad one detective to eliminate and why."

I collected the papers from everyone, and then I read the person and the reason.

"Andrew, because he has such a large family, which might need his attention."

"Detective Andrew Capozzoli, as he may retire once he reaches twenty-five years on the force."

"Andrew Capozzoli, because of his age."

"Detective Capozzoli, again because of his family and age."

"Detective Capozzoli; since he is one of the best, he will be missed as a detective."

"Two more votes against Andrew Capozzoli, because of his large family. That concludes all the votes," I said.

"Okay, it was unanimous, Detective Andrew Capozzoli for various reasons. Remember that what is said in our meetings stays in the meetings. Now please cast your vote for our new team member," David said. It only took a minute.

I looked at all the votes. All seven votes were for Paula Hand.

Big John asked, "Why did everyone like Paula?"

"She is the youngest detective, making her more willing to learn and easy to train in the way we work," Tender explained.

"I also believe Jane Woodward, being just married might become a problem, as we never know when we will have to leave and go on assignment," added Mary.

"I voted for Paula thinking along the same lines as Mary. I was also thinking about the times we have meetings at our home without pay, which is necessary. Chief Purdy has agreed to allow the new hire to attend meetings and receive a reward from us, but they will receive no hourly pay from the police department unless they are on police duty," I said.

"We will need to vote on hiring Detective Paula Hand and giving her a percentage of our rewards," David said. "All in favor, raise your right hand." Everyone raised their hand in approval.

David said, "The matter is approved." I finished up the minutes of our meeting and placed them in our business meeting binder. Then David handed out checks to John, Mary and Richard. David had Richard and Mary sign each check and said he would deposit it on Monday for them.

It was a wonderful, restful weekend. We had beautiful weather and lots of fun with our family.

We informed Chief Purdy that we had chosen Detective Paula Hand. He would inform Detective Paula and post the news on the bulletin board on Monday.

On Monday, we headed to FBI headquarters to review the new case. Tender received her rainbow pop from the front desk, and we headed up to the seventh floor.

We all went right into action, studying the

pictures and the evidence. Tender and Vicky stayed next to each other, and Vicky asked a lot of questions. Finally, Tender spoke up.

"So, as I understand, you are calling this the 'Mechanic Killer' case?" Tender asked.

"Yes, because he leaves a wrench with every dead body," Agent Sisson said grimly.

"I noticed a drop of blood on every wrench. I wonder why it's blood, and if it's the blood of the victims?" Tender noticed.

"No it is probably not," responded Agent Sisson.

"I see that we have 1/4", 5/16", and 3/8". We are missing 7/16" and 1/2", and then we have 9/16" and 5/8". So, we need to find the bodies for the two missing wrenches, and the next ones will be 11/16", up to 1". I pray he will stop at the 1" wrench," Tender said.

"We need to stop this 'Mechanic Killer,' as he probably has six more murders planned before he will stop!" I exclaimed.

"Now, why is he leaving a wrench, Tender?" asked Agent Sisson.

"Let me guess, you have a feeling he works for a car dealership or a car repair place, like a gas station," I guessed. Tender nodded and gave me a thumbs-up.

"Yes, we have called every dealership in the

area where we found the bodies," Agent Sisson responded.

"Okay, team, what do you see?" asked Tender.

"Well, first of all, wrenches as small as 1/4" would never be used at a car repair facility," said David.

"Correct. It would be like a specialty shop. Perhaps a carburetor rebuilding shop, a transmission shop, or a generator/alternator rebuilding facility. It could also be a voltage regulator shop or radio repair shop. These are nationwide, like Peterson transmission company," Tender answered. Everyone just stood there trying to decide what we needed to do first.

*Join Tender Purdy in her next book
and see if she can stop the 'Mechanic Killer'
before he uses all his wrenches.*

About the Author

Richard P. Harrington grew up in the inner city in Providence, Rhode Island. Struggling through school and graduating with only a fifth-grade education made writing difficult. Richard worked for many years as a builder and cabinet maker before pursuing his life-long dream of writing mysteries. In 2021 Richard began dreaming each night about a little girl named Tender Purdy. His story comes to life as he uses real life events to write his intriguing stories.

tenderpurdymysteries@gmail.com

Made in the USA
Middletown, DE
11 May 2024

54120694R00149